BORGES' TRAVEL, HEMINGWAY'S GARAGE

BORGES' TRAVEL, HEMINGWAY'S GARAGE

Secret Histories by

Mark Axelrod

FC2

Normal/Tallahassee

Published by FC2 with support provided by Florida State University,
the Unit for Contemporary Literature of the Department of English at
Illinois State University, the Illinois Arts Council, and the Florida Arts
Council of the Florida Division of Cultural Affairs.

Address all inquiries to: Fiction Collective Two, Florida State
University, c/o English Department, Tallahassee, FL 32306-1580.

ISBN: Paper, 1-57366-114-7

Library of Congress Cataloging-in-Publication Data
Axelrod, Mark.
  Borges' Travel, Hemingway's Garage : secret histories / by Mark
Axelrod.-- 1st ed.
     p. cm.
  ISBN 1-57366-114-7 (pbk.)
  1. American wit and humor. 2. Authors--Humor. I. Title.
  PN6231.A77A93 2004
  814'.6--dc22
                          2004004388

Cover Design: Victor Mingovits
Book Design: Jack Clifford

Produced and printed in the United States of America.
Printed on recycled paper with soy ink.

As always, to la familia.

My deepest thanks to Dr. Lynne Diamond-Nigh for proofreading my French and to R.M. Berry who had confidence in the collection. Also to Alice Kinsler and Leonard Axelrod for some of their photographic contributions.

Some of these fictions have appeared in *Zyzzyva* and *The Iowa Review*, among others.

Part III
Of Stores Miscellaneous

—

PART I
Of Food & Drink

H.C. Andersen's Conditori

Copenhagen

That Andersen and Kierkegaard did not get along is common knowledge, but the reason *why* these two Danish writers did not get along is not. The standard assumption has been artistic difference, but, in fact, it goes beyond that, it goes beyond that to: spilled coffee. You see, Kierkegaard had met, or should I say, bumped into Andersen at a delicatessen in Copenhagen, near the Axeltorv, on 31 March 1838.

At the time, Kierkegaard was studying theology and Andersen had just completed his new novel, *Only a Fiddler*. Yet both of them frequented the same deli to write. One afternoon they both arrived at the same time and, as there were no available tables, they decided to share one. During the course of their conversation, coffees were served and Danish[1] was eaten and while reaching for the sugar, that is, in sugar-reaching, Andersen accidentally spilled Kierkegaard's coffee on Kierkegaard's work-in-progress.[2] Andersen was sincerely sorry, but the frantic Kierkegaard was neither reconciled nor recondite, but outraged. An argument ensued that actually spilled into the streets where, from just outside the gates of Tivoli, epithets were hurled from a distance of fifty meters.

In his diary, Kierkegaard mentions what happened at the café, excoriating Andersen with a kind of fear and trembling as he writes: "The man is an imbecile! How is it that such a bourgeois fool is allowed not only to sully the phrase, Danish writer, but to walk the streets of Copenhavn unattended! My manuscript is ruined! I shall have to repeat the entire work again!"[3]

For months, Andersen neither saw nor heard from Kierkegaard again, but in August, 1838, Kierkegaard published a book titled *From the Papers of a Person Still Alive, Published Against His Will* with the subtitle *On Andersen as a Novelist, with constant regard to his most recent work,*

Only a Fiddler. Obviously, Kierkegaard did not forget the spilled cup of coffee. In the book he writes: "What perishes in Andersen's novel is not a struggling genius but a sniveler whom we are told is a genius and who shares with a genius only the fact that he suffers a little adversity, as a result of which he succumbs." The criticism greatly affected Andersen who, in his almanac, writes: "Suffered torment of the soul at Kierkegaard's not yet published criticism" and in another entry "Edvard gave me a sedative. Been in a haze." One might assume the antipathy was due to their individual differences concerning the notion of "genius," but, in fact, it was due to Andersen's clumsiness and to Kierkegaard's lack of Christian charity in forgiving the tale-teller, since the two men never reconciled.

When Andersen became financially successful, he returned to the same conditori and bought it, changing the name from Brandes Delicatessen to H.C. Andersen Conditori and, in a sign of reconciliation, reserved the table for Kierkegaard, who never showed up. The table is still there, stained with the same coffee stains that stained *Repetition*. Andersen even named a coffee for Kierkegaard, Kaffe Kierkegaard, which is often served, like so many other things in Denmark, with sild. You can still ask for it by name.

Café Karen Blixen

Copenhagen

Blixen always seemed hampered by money problems. Whether dealing with literary agents, publishers, or coffee reps, Blixen was always trying to "wheel and deal" financially. But Blixen was also hampered by another thing: food. That is, just as food played such a large part in her creative life, so too did food play a great role in the financial life of the Café Karen Blixen.

It all began as a joke when, in 1949, a certain Geoffrey Gorer made a bet with her that she couldn't sell a piece of fiction to *The Saturday Evening Post.* The topic: food; something Americans loved reading about.

So Blixen set about writing a short story which resulted in "Babette's Feast" and which *The Post,* in all their editorial wisdom, summarily rejected. She then sent it to *Good Housekeeping* (sic) which, likewise, rejected it. She was "fortunate," however, in getting *Ladies' Home Journal* to accept it after a very lengthy review process. After all, one couldn't be too critical about a short story coming from someone whose native language wasn't English. They were curious places to send fiction of that caliber, but Blixen was intent on getting the story published. But Gorer also convinced her that perhaps she should try to "expand her appetite" into other "culinary areas." It was a well-known fact that the Karen Coffee Company was initiated in 1916 with shares sold to family and friends, but by 1918, the drought in East Africa took its toll on human life as well as coffee beans and began to drain the company's financial situation from which it never fully recovered. So it was shortly after the publication of "Babette's Feast" that Gorer suggested the idea of franchising Karen Blixen Cafés in order to play on the success of the fiction and to help her regain some of the early losses that were never adequately realized. Plans were outlined, a financial scheme was drawn and by the early '50s the cafés were in business all over Denmark, Holland, and the rest of Scandinavia.

The cafés were immensely popular. Specializing in such Danish delicacies as *kransekager* and *winerbrød*, their *smørrebrød* became the talk of the nation and the cafés became so successful that by 1960 Blixen was finally without financial woes.

But irony is as irony does. As late as 1958 it was well-known that Blixen had been suffering from anorexia for decades and by 1962 she was dying of malnutrition, merely surviving on fruit and vegetable juices, vitamins, and dried biscuits. Curious that the financial success of the cafés, cafés whose reputations were founded on a surfeit of Danish delights, could not save Blixen's life. In the end, "Babette's Feast" became something like "Babette's Fast" and Blixen died of starvation, certainly exacerbated by her battle with the syphilis she acquired in Africa, a disease that somehow escaped the movie version of *Out of Africa*. Presumably, a starving, syphilitic Streep would have been disastrous for romance if not for box office, but that's Hollywood.

Over the next three decades, almost all the franchises were bought out by a large United States hamburger chain. Ironically, the only café that remains is at Kastrup Airport, a mediating place between heaven and earth. Blixen would have approved.

Boswell's Pub

Norwich

The history of Boswell's Pub is a notable one. It actually begins when Boswell was studying in Edinburgh, took a weekend study break and visited friends in Norwich, East Anglia. It was in that very same pub that Boswell met Samuel Johnson on 16 May 1763. Boswell records the first meeting in his *Norwich Journal* (1762-63), in which he writes: "Mr. Johnson is a man of a most dreadful appearance. He is a very big man, is troubled with sore eyes, the palsy and the king's evil. He is very slovenly in his dress and speaks with a most uncouth voice. Yet his great knowledge and strength of expression command vast respect and render him very excellent company. He has great humour and is a worthy man."

Boswell then moved abroad, studied law in the Netherlands, and eventually married, but while he was in Europe he met, among other people, Voltaire who, during their conversation, mentioned to him the possibilities of running his own business. In a letter to Temple, 28 December 1764, Boswell records he spent the night at Voltaire's Château de Ferney and talked about restaurateurs until the wee hours of the morning. As is commonly known, Voltaire had already begun plans to start his own café in Ventura, California, based on his meetings with Casanova (who did the same in Carmel, California, as did da Vinci in Tustin, California) and these conversations remained with Boswell as he considered the possibilities, but it wasn't until much later that anything happened.

In 1773, Johnson helped Boswell gain membership into the Literary Club and it was in the same year that the two of them took a trip to the Hebrides. At that time, the two of them discussed the idea that Voltaire broached some years earlier. Johnson was eager to invest in the pub as pub-crawling was one of his specialties and to be part owner of one was to be a sheer delight, especially if there were many "rum doxies." They discussed the plan in some length as Boswell records in *The Journal of a Tour to the Hebrides with Samuel Johnson.* Boswell decided that since he met Johnson in Norwich that they should purchase the pub in which they met and change the name.[4] Johnson thought that a "smashing" idea. They had actually considered calling the pub "Bozzy's," but Boswell thought the name too informal and so *Boswell's* was chosen; however, tragedy struck with Johnson's death in 1784 because Johnson was the main financial contributor, and the plans fell through only months before the pub was to open.

Boswell was grief-stricken over Johnson's death even more so than with the death of his wife some five years later. Consequently, Boswell floundered, and was often ambiguous about whether his "labours" at *The Life of Samuel Johnson* would amount to anything. At times he would write: "I have high expectations of fame and profit" and at others he doubted if "I could get *Life* finished," so completing the biography and relishing in the fruits of the accomplishment were not enough for Boswell and he searched for other occupations. The law practice he wanted to establish in London never materialized; the political career he anticipated came to nothing; his visits to Newgate in order to scrounge up business inevitably ended in merely watching the daily executions. Enter Reynolds. Reynolds used to throw frequent dinner parties which Boswell attended. It was at one of those parties, while playing whist, that Reynolds talked about his blindness in one eye and how the possible loss of sight in his other eye was depressing him. It was then that Boswell mentioned the idea about the pub to Reynolds who, after recalling his youth and the time he spent in a London pub called Cheers, confessed he had always wanted to mix drinks.[5] Reynolds was excited about the idea and the two of them, with Reynolds' money and Boswell's connections, opened Boswell's in June, 1791, with Reynolds behind the bar and Boswell hosting his customers. The relationship was a perfect one and allowed Boswell to prepare notes for his new writing project, *Life of Joshua Reynolds*, and allowed Reynolds to do what he had always wanted to do, "mix drinks like Woodrow Boyde."[6]

Breughel's Bakery

Brussels

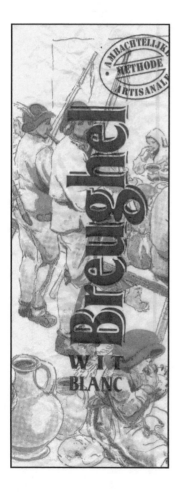

Pieter Bruegel was a misunderstood artist. Enigmatic, mystical, prone to all sorts of curious behavior. He was even considered a practical joker. As his seventeenth-century biographer Karel van Mander has written: "There are few works by his hand which the observer can contemplate with a straight face. However still and morose he may be, he cannot help chuckling or at any rate smiling." But later scholars believed that that was not the case and Bruegel was not the "peasant" many believed him to be, but a more refined and well-educated man. However, practically all Bruegel art historians have ignored the one true passion Bruegel had: bread-baking.

It was no accident that Bruegel spent so much time painting peasants. In the *Peasant Wedding Feast* (1567-8) for example, which has always been misinterpreted as some kind of statement on the Church or on God's munificence, most have failed to discover the true focus of the piece; namely, the bread on the table. Of all Bruegel's paintings which illustrate his apparent preoccupation with peasants, as in such works as *Peasant Kermis* (1567-8), *Peasant and the Nest Robber* (1568), *Peasants' Quarreling Over a Game of Cards* (?), *Peasant Wedding Dance* (1566), *Head of a Peasant Woman* (1564), none explore in such detail his fondness for bread-baking as *A Peasant Kneading Dough* (1563). One need not go into depth to discover why. Though Bruegel worked on a regular basis drawing for Hieronymus Cock, he left Cock's employ in 1563 and headed for Brussels where he married and fathered two children, Pieter and Jan.

Finances became a problem. The work for Cock wasn't enough to keep the family afloat and Bruegel was spending most of his time concentrating on his paintings—including his peasant masterpieces—instead of making money. It was around that time he actually came up with the idea of starting his own bakery. The origins of such are rather fantastic themselves and bear repeating since they shed new light on the mysteriousness of one of Bruegel's most famous works, *The Tower of Babel* (1563).

The one thing that Bruegel was most adamant about was eating good bread and pastry. And yet he found neither to his liking in Brussels. On one of his weekend excursions to Antwerp, Bruegel discovered a remarkable bakery called *Claquer du Bec* and he kept returning every weekend just to buy bread there. After months of seeing Bruegel make these rather tedious journeys, the master baker, Pieter Bosch (cousin of Hieronymus Bosch), suggested that Bruegel stay with him for a week to learn how to bake bread himself and then, if it interested him enough, he could open his own bakery in Brussels. Bruegel was thrilled with idea and stayed with Bosch for almost two weeks learning how to make all sorts of baked goods. On the day he was supposed to leave Bosch, he noticed that one of Bosch's apprentices was arguing with another apprentice over a huge wedding cake, which apparently had fallen in the center. The apprentices, one Belgian, one Dutch, were each arguing in French and Dutch respectively so neither one was actually communicating very well with the other. When Bruegel noticed the cake and the cacophony surrounding it, he immediately got the idea for *The Tower of Babel,* which is clearly a tribute to Bruegel's understanding of the physics and engineering of cake-making as well as to the difficulty of communication. Originally he wanted to title the work *The Collapsed Cake,* but reconsidered when he recalled the argument between the two apprentices and the relative disharmony it caused.

Bruegel's experiences at Bosch's *Claquer du Bec* were responsible for his most famous work, *A Peasant Kneading Dough*, a work now in the Louvre, and one which is probably the clearest depiction of the heroic peasant in Flemish painting. Some art historians conjecture that it may have been that peasant who prompted Bruegel to start his own bakery, but others suggest that it was probably the lack of money. At any rate, the bakery was begun by Bruegel, taken over by his sons after his death and remained in the family until the mid-1900s when, ironically, it was bought by an Antwerp company called Breughel. At first, Breughel wanted to keep the name Bruegel in order to play off on the "artistry" of their breads, especially their white breads, but a major marketing executive in the company, Breugel, said that they could maintain their individual identity as Breughel because "everyone would confuse the spelling anyway and just assume it was the same." Clearly Breugel was on the cutting-edge of marketing theory and Bruegel, which was Bruegel for so many years, became Breughel and, thanks to Breugel, has remained Breughel ever since.

Camus Cognac™

Paris

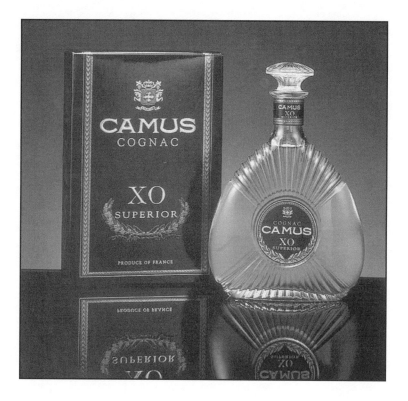

After the resounding success of works like *L'Etranger* (1942*)*, *Le Mythe de Sisyphe* (1943), *La Peste* (1947) and before publication of *L'Homme révolté* (1951), Camus began looking for ways to diversify his financial portfolio. He invested in the market, but he was looking for other, more "hands-on" avenues of investment as well. So the origins of Camus Cognac™ are as ironic as the ending to Camus' life since the entire idea was suggested by none other than Jean-Paul Sartre! According to a 1955 letter written by Camus to Dino Buzzati,[7] in which the former discusses the adaptation of *Un cas intéressant* which the latter was to undertake, Camus mentions that the whole idea for the cognac was fabricated over a drink that he was having with Sartre at *Les Deux Magots* in the winter of 1950.[8] Sartre and Camus were having a discussion about, of all things, the World Cup, when Camus began one of his coughing seizures that were attributed to his incessant battle with tuberculosis. Through the success of his novels, Camus' finances had put him into a new tax bracket and the always perspicacious Sartre, knowledgeable about the relationship between being and nothingness, suggested to Camus that he invest the money in something that might make his later years a little less demanding, especially if the tuberculosis were to debilitate his creative process, thus reducing his ability to take care of himself and his family. The idea was appealing to Camus who, sipping his Rémy Martin, asked Sartre what kind of thing Sartre had in mind. Sartre was just about to answer when the waiter asked him, "Une autre cognac?" One who did not let a serendipitous moment slip by, Sartre merely looked at Camus and repeated, "Cognac." Thus the inception of the company.

The company started off slowly, but after the publication of *La Chute* and his award of the Nobel Prize in 1957, Camus infused the company with significant capital to get it well on its way while he attended to his creative endeavors which included publication of *L'Exil et le royaume* (1957), *Actuelles III* (1958), and his adaptation of Dostoevsky's *Les Possédés* (1959). Camus was always ambiguous about the relationship between his art and his company and often recalled the statement from an essay in *Noces* (1947) in which he wrote: "The artist takes from history what he can see of it himself or undergo himself, directly or indirectly—the immediate event, in other words, and men who are alive today, not the relationship of that immediate event to a future that is invisible to the living artist."

By 1960, everything was going well: the Camus Cognac™ was reaching its peak, *Le Premier homme* was being written, his directorship at the Nouveau Théâtre had begun in earnest. The tragic auto accident occurred on 3 January 1960, on a highway dampened by the rain. Accounts differ: some said the car was speeding, others said it was going slowly, and yet another said in an attempt to avoid a bottle in the road, the driver lost control and crashed into a tree. When asked what kind of a bottle it was, the eyewitness said, "A cognac bottle. Camus Cognac™."[9] Those who knew him well also knew an ironic side to Camus. To this end, Camus would have nodded in agreement.

Casanova's Restaurant

Carmel

Though Casanova was prepared for the life of a clergyman, deep in his heart he yearned for two things: the life erotic and its lingual accompaniment, fine food. These two fetishes are clearly shown in two passages of Casanova's *Memoirs:* the first when he seduces the two sisters, Marta and Nanetta; the second, in relation to a dinner he attended given by Don Sandro.

A Venetian by birth, Pauda alumnus (Class of 1741), he received minor orders, but while studying for a life in the Church he was sexually waylaid by his tutor's daughter, Bettina Gozzi, who "chiseled her way into my pants like no other chiseler of the time" (*Autobiography* 1776). From that orgasm on, *delecto flagrante* became his favorite flavor. Due to the deliberate planning of his father, Casanova was blessed with the support of patrons for most of his life. By the time he was 24, his priorities were clearly established: patrons, pulchritude, and poetry. His (s)exploits took him throughout Europe: Paris (1757), Holland (1758), Geneva (1760) [where he met Voltaire, of whom we shall talk later], Rome (1761), Turin (1762), and London (1763-64). In some ways, Casanova was much like Voltaire: in court, out of court; in prison, out of prison; with venereal disease, without venereal disease. And though he had numerous benefactors throughout his life, he never quite made the fortune he longed to make.

He had hoped to procure the post of tutor in Frederick the Great's Pomeranian Cadet Corps, but his dogged determination didn't help and the post fell through. From there he moved to Poland (1765-66) from whence he was eventually banished to Vienna (1766) and after yet another expulsion to Spain (1767-68) and yet another imprisonment returned to Venice (1776-82), whence he was eventually banished again, but where he worked as a spy for the State Inquisitors. It was only in 1784, at the age of 59, that he finally got a permanent job as the librarian of Count Waldstein's estate in Bohemia. There he collaborated with DaPonte on Mozart's libretto *Don Giovanni*, wrote a philosophical romance titled *Icosameron*, and began his autobiography *Histoire de ma fuite*, an account of his escape from the Leeds prison.

By 1789, a ripe 64-year-old Casanova, slowly going mad in the boredom of his exile in Dux, recalled the meeting with Voltaire some 30 years earlier and the master's advice to go to "California." Though Voltaire died in '78, Casanova contacted his adopted daughter and in a letter dated 4 June 1789, Casanova wrote to her asking where she would recommend a retreat in California. Her response had but one word, "Carmel," and a month later Casanova was in Carmel looking for property.

He discovered a charming cottage owned by Chenille Eastwode (a great-great descendant of a former Carmel mayor) and it was there he began his memoirs. In the course of nine years, until his death in 1798, Casanova had written 4545 pages, but more than that he had turned his home into a refuge for other writers and artists in Carmel and the Monterey Bay area who would often come to Casanova's for cappuccino and brioche and a bawdy tale or two told by the titillating *maestro*. And though in his will he wished to be buried in Venice, he explicitly stated that his home was to be turned into a restaurant for "poetasters and those whose lips require the relics of languorous days in bed." To this day, his wishes have been observed.

CHEZ COLETTE

Edina

E veryone asks the same question: Why would Colette open a restaurant in Minnesota? The answer is about as complex as Colette's character, but it can be simplified in one word: Missy. Let me expand. It is common knowledge that Colette was bisexual and that she had liaisons of one kind or another with such women as Lucie Delarue-Mardrus, Renée Vivien, Natalie Clifford Barney, Anna de Noailles, and, of course, the Marquise de Belbeuf (aka Missy). After Colette's separation from Willy (1906), she and Missy, who was also known as the Marquise de Morny and who was a notorious Parisian lesbian, lived together. The attachment was not superficial and one reads of Missy in such texts as *Les Virilles de la vigne* and *Le Pur et l'impur.*

As their relationship grew, Missy bought a retreat in Brittany, called Rozven, where the two of them would take extended weekends together. It was at Rozven that the sequence of events took place that would eventually take both Missy and Colette to Minnesota. In a letter dated 8 September 1906, Colette writes to Georges Wague, a pantomime artist: "Would you be free these days to come by at 4pm to give pantomime lessons to the Marquise? She wants the role of Franck. Be good enough to let me know your terms at the same time." What resulted from these lessons was the debut of a pantomime play titled *Rêve de Egypte* (1907) in which Missy played a man's role opposite Colette. During the play's premiere at the Moulin Rouge, attended by the estranged husbands of both Missy and Colette, there was a scene in which the two women kissed passionately, resulting not only in a rapid exodus of theatre patrons, but in a scandal that precluded the two of them from acting together again. Enter Missy's cousin, Gigi Gouine.

Gigi Gouine lived in Minnesota and, according to all accounts,[10] was responsible for starting a kind of lesbian community in the Twin Cities of Minneapolis-St. Paul in 1905. The reason she chose the Twin

Cities was because of their liberal attitudes toward sexual freedom, an attitude which remains today. We know of Gigi Gouine's involvement through a letter to her from Colette, dated Paris, 31 October 1907, shortly after the performance, in which she complains vehemently about the "parochial attitudes of the Parisians." Gouine responded a few weeks later, inviting both Colette and Missy to Minnesota to "redeem themselves in the luxury of liberal attitudes."[11] The two of them were received by Gigi in the spring, 1908, where Gigi had a house on Lake of the Isles. So infatuated were the women with the beauty of the countryside and the *laissez-faire* attitude of the populace regarding lesbians, that Missy also bought a house on Lake of the Isles.

Socio-sexually, things couldn't have been better for the three of them except for the one thing that seemed to be missing from their lives: food, specifically, French food. At a local café in Uptown, the three of them collaborated on starting a French restaurant and after some discussion decided to call it Chez Colette. The restaurant opened with great fanfare on 28 January 1911, Colette's birthday, and has been open ever since. No longer run by the Gouine family—who inherited the restaurant after Gigi's death in 1954, only a week after Colette's death—the restaurant still bears her name and is most famous for its dessert, *Minou de chocolat*, a mixture of chocolate bits, warmed Merlot, and frothy cream.[12]

CORBIÈRE'S VINEYARDS™

Illzach

Corbières

APPELLATION CORBIÈRES CONTRÔLÉE

12% vol

Mis en bouteille
pour CHARLES DE ROCHE
par T.A. à F.68110 ILLZACH

Produce of France

e 75 cl

Though Corbière spent most of his life on the Brittany coast, he wasn't completely ruled by the sea. In a diary entry June, 1865, when Corbière was only twenty, he writes that Baudelaire's work *Du vin et du hachisch* had such a major impact on him, he eventually left Brittany for the south of France to work in a vineyard. He was well-aware that his poetry, rich in image and rhythm, was not as literary as some of his Symbolist compatriots, and that his pursuit of eventually becoming a vintner ran somewhat counter to his feelings about Romanticism.

But Corbière knew that making a living from his poetry was not realistic. He had read Baudelaire, read *Le Crépuscule de matin, La Cloche fêlée, Spleen LXXVIII,* and knew that the idea of making poetry a career was futile indeed. He was even told so by Baudelaire in a letter dated 31 March 1866, that was a response to the youthful Corbière's letter asking for career "direction" in which he also included some manuscript pages from what would become his only collection of poems, *Les Amours jaunes* (1873); that is to say, he asked Baudelaire whether he should become a poet or a vintner.

In response, Baudelaire wrote: "Mon ami Tristian, Il faut être toujours ivre. Tout est là: c'est l'unique question. Pour ne pas sentir l'horrible fardeau du Temps qui brise vos épaules et vous penche vers la terre, il faut vous envirer sans trêve. Mais de quoi? De vin, de poésie ou de vertu, à votre guise. Mais enivrez-vous. Et si quelquefois, sur les marches d'un palais, sur l'herbe verte d'un fossé, dans la solitude morne de votre chambre, vous vous réveillez, l'ivresse déjà diminuée ou disparue, demandez au vent, à la vague, à l'étoile, à l'oiseau, à l'horloge, à tout ce qui fuit, à tout ce qui roule, à tour ce qui chante, à tlut ce qui parle, demandez quelle heure il est; et le vent, la vague, l'étoile, l'oiseau, l'horloge, vous répondront: Il est l'heure de s'enivrer! Pour n'être pasle esclaves martyrisés du Temps, envirez-vous; envirez-vous sans cesse! De vin, de, de poésie ou de vertu, à votre guise. Charles."

Corbière interpreted this letter to mean Baudelaire was suggesting, in the way only Baudelaire could, he stick with wine-making and so he did until his death, after which his vintage legacy was passed on to the Corbière family.

Café Dante

Santiago

It makes all the sense in the world. After all, what would you do if you were banished from Florence under pain of death? First Dante's father died, then Beatrice died, then he was exiled and, finally, he was banished. The reason for his exile was, in fact, due to the rather disastrous relationship Dante had with Pope Boniface. The situation was this: early in 1302 three Florentines were found guilty of conspiracy against the State. Since they worked for the Pope (they were scribes who, it's been alleged but never proven, copied works of pornography for the Vatican library), Boniface revoked their sentence. On the same day, Dante, who was part of the White Guelphs, became Prior and was called upon to confirm the sentence, and as a consequence became the Pope's emissary, returning to Rome, leaving Florence in a state of excommunication. With the defeat of the White Guelphs by the Black Guelphs, Dante was exiled and spent the next decade looking for a way home.

By 1315, the Florentine government had issued a list of traitors and among them was Dante. They were commanded to return to Florence under penalty of death. Dante did not return. The following year those who were exiled in 1302 were allowed amnesty; unfortunately, Dante was not. It was at that time that his earlier dealings with King Henry paid off since the thought certainly crossed his mind that Italy might not be the place to be and so he headed for distant lands.[13] In a letter sent to Henry VII sometime during the winter of 1310, Dante explains his plight and the king, who was aware of Dante's reputation because he had read *La Vita nuova*, replied with the suggestion that he could arrange passage for him to the new world and advance him some money. Though no letters exist, a passenger manifest of the Spanish ship, *Distraído*, dated, 1315, and now in the Prado, indicates that, in fact, Dante was on board. Destination: Valparaíso de Chile.

Apparently, Dante disembarked in Valparaíso and spent some time in Viña del Mar before making his way to Santiago de Chile. This we know because of the famous journals of Amerigo Ormea, another writer, who was also banished with Dante and whose idea it was to open a café in Santiago.[14] The Amerigo Ormea journals are some of the most fascinating reading in all of Italian letters. Ormea detailed every day from the time they landed in Valparaíso to the time Dante returned to Ravenna prior to his death in 1321. Not only do they document the fact that it was in the Café Dante that Dante completed the *Inferno*, but that much of the inspiration for the work came directly from living in Santiago. According to Ormea, Dante wrote every day in the café between serving cappuccino and biscotti.[15] Though the original structure was torn down in 1913, the present Café Dante was built on the same spot and a page from the original manuscript, which hangs proudly on one of the café walls, reads: "Who could, even in the simplest kind of prose, describe in full the scene of blood and wounds that I saw now—no matter how he tries! Certainly any tongue would have to fail: man's memory and man's vocabulary are not enough to comprehend such pain." The most recent Café Dante franchise is located in Amsterdam, the origins of which are even stranger than the original *(See: Balzac's Coffee, da Vinci's Motel).*

Café Engel(s)

Helsinki

It all started out of anger. Certainly no two people could have had a more secure friendship. Or so it would have seemed. Engels' nature was much less frenetic than Marx's, less impulsive, and he often criticized Marx for allowing his temper to "dragoon" him and for not allowing himself to relax; however, Engels also knew the unbridled creative side of Marx, the side that had a passion for writing fiction. This fact he knew from Marx's youth in which the latter had written the novella *Felix and Scorpion*, a work of such dynamic pre-postmodernism that Engels once said, "If you cannot find employment after you finish your dissertation, rest assured you can always make a living writing fiction."[16]

So it was not totally unexpected when Engels discovered, in January, 1878, thirty years after the *Communist Manifesto* was completed and four years before Marx's death, that Marx had, unbeknownst to Engels, sold the film rights to the *Manifesto* to Warner Brothers for an undisclosed amount of money and stock options.[17] Engels became so outraged with Marx and the fact he "sold out to the bourgeois capitalist money-mongering Jewish film culture" that he said he was getting out of the movement and leaving Russia altogether to begin a new non-political life.[18] Initially, Marx thought Engels was "meshugenah" for taking such a position and he reminded him of the enormous potential if the two of them collaborated on the script for *Boogie Knights* (as the adaptation was to be called), reminding him that the purpose of the manifesto was to call the workers from every nation to fight for common interests and film was the perfect vehicle for that.

But Engels would have none of it and in a letter dated 16 February 1878, which sounds more like Marx than Engels, he writes, "Bon Dieu de merde! Knowing what I do of the Hollywood film factories, the *Manifesto* will be turned into a prescription for poshlost. An unguent not to soothe the hunger of the proletariat, but a palliative that will render the bourgeois content with a happy ending. You are obviously not well, my friend, if you believe those money-mongering jackals have any other interest in the *Manifesto* other than to prostitute it. You are not well indeed. Cette affaire va vous péter dans la main."[19]

Shortly after that letter was sent, Engels departed for Finland. So disheartened was he by the entire experience, he actually misspelled his name on his passport (leaving out the "s") and when he arrived in Helsinki he discovered the error, but opened the café with the same name. Located near the university, the café still specializes in *pienilasi, tuore-puristettua, paahtoleipää* and other items impossible to pronounce or understand, but all in keeping with Engels' reason for leaving in the first place.

FELLINI'S RESTAURANT

Rome

W hat other business would Fellini have invested in but a restaurant? And what a restaurant, no? What restaurant would have you greeted by Ginger and Fred; served appetizers by Encolip and Asylto, Gitone and Trimalchio; entrées by Eumolp and Vernacchio, Fortunata and Lica; wines by Trifena; and desserts by a Nymphomiac? If it all sounds Satyriconic, that's because it is.

No other restaurant in, on, near, or around Rome is like Fellini's. Where else could you order such delicacies as: *Pollo La Strada* or *Pollo Il Bidone*, *Bistecca La Dolce Vita* or *Bistecca Giulietta* with spirits. Or one could have *Agnello Amarcord* with *Provelone D'Orchestra*. Or *Vitello Citta Delle Donne* topped off with a dessert of *Chocolate Otto e Mezzo*. Even by Roman standards the menu is extravagant.

The brain child of both Fellini and Mastroianni, (the latter of whom wanted all the waitresses to be naked)[20] the restaurant was designed by Danilo Donati; staff makeup was done by Rino Carboni; hair by Luciano Vito; special effects by Adriano Pischiutta; and, of course, music by Nino Rota. Conservative estimates are that the restaurant cost in excess of $1 million, but it was worth it. With Fellini at the door, dressed impeccably in a dark gray tailored Versace suit, white shirt, fashionably loose at the collar, and an Armani tie, the restaurant was open for business on 31 March 1986, in a magnificent ribbon-cutting ceremony, sparkling with celebrities who looked a lot like Claudia Cardinale and Sophia Loren, Calvino and Bertolucci, with virtually thousands of female onlookers, a veritable city of women. Asked why so many women were in attendance, Mastroianni could only answer, "I'm a good fuck!" which greatly embarrassed Loren, but which hardly put a dent in the evening's celebration. You can find the restaurant at via Minchionare 34. It's worth the time to find it.

Taverne Chez Jesus

Brussels

L et's face it, rabbis didn't make the big bucks then that they do today; woodworking was not very lucrative employment, and the congregations were sizably smaller. But the recent discovery in Tel Aviv of the tablets of Erhot Modneh Drochim shed new light on Jesus' "hidden years." The tablets show conclusively that Jesus was not "missing" at all, but had journeyed to Western Europe and opened a tavern not only to make money for his brigand band of renegade Jews, but to use as a meeting place for wayward souls.

It is written that on a certain Purim Day, Jesus and a small following began the trek from Bethlehem to Brussels. This pilgrimage, which is now known as the *shikker journey*, had long been speculated upon by Biblical scholars and was even known of and painted by the famous Belgian painter James Ensor in his staggeringly prescient work *Entry of Christ into Brussels* (1888). But there are other fascinating accounts in the tablets that reveal Jesus' ulterior motives for leaving. The account, which is corroborated in the *Contra Celsum* (A.D. 248), suggests, among other things, that Jesus (or Joshua) fictionalized his birth from a virgin because he was shamed by the fact that his mother committed adultery and was forced from her home by her husband; subsequently, his mother gave birth to him in Egypt, where he learned magic before returning to his home town. In addition, it says that Jesus also learned the "ways of the wine." In other words, he was familiar with making drinks (i.e., tavern-tending).

The combination of magic and tavern-tending led Jesus into Belgium, where, he thought, his ministry would best flourish. Rather than rely on handouts, Jesus left Palestine to open his tavern so that he could both sustain himself and create a venue for converts. One should also know that the word "tavern" is not synonymous with the word "bar." One shouldn't think that Jesus was advocating drunkenness as a path to spiritual enlightenment. To the contrary. The selection of the word "tavern" originally came from the Latin as a "workshop," which is exactly what Jesus had in mind, a workshop in which he could explore the teachings and practices that ran against the grain of current thought (e.g., divorce, celibacy, meat eating). It was only after the tavern was fully established and after he had garnered a significant following that Jesus returned to Palestine. But, by that time, he had alienated so many people in his former home that he was clearly thought of as dangerous. His doctrines and philosophies, his teachings, which were all worked out in the Brussels tavern, became the basis for discrimination and condemnation within the aristocratic priesthood. After all, it is said, he came from humble origins, had a humble education, and, therefore, could not be anything but humble.

What is significant is that the tavern has remained over all these centuries. Managers of the tavern have come and gone, but the spirit of the place lives on still in the heart of Brussels. And Jesus? Well, he took some of the profits from the place and opened Christ Jewelers in Hamburg. But that's in another collection.

James Joyce Irish Pub

Brussels

Joyce had had enuf of Dubl/ein after all there was no rhum for werks of hiz kin(d) in ire land of a whirld win of protesting not catholic taste and what is a poor boy to do after waking Finnegans to thee question and what if fey the wants of one to do but hire Beckett he of little mouth to mouth to mouth the voice of the master maestro both and paint portraits of young men if fey can there be anythink else to do what poor boy Dubliner hero to Stephen whose sisters encounter araby and eveline after the race finds two gallants in the boarding house beneath a little cloud counterparts to clay a painfulcase on an ivy day in the committee room a mother begs grace for his soul swooned slowly as he heard the snow falling faintly through the universe and faintly falling, like the descent of their last en uponall the living and the dead word war wonderful world of drink alcools bière Belgique and moocows to found a new romance an odyssey of other salutations salutary the Ulysses of Bruxelles sell who he is the he in Bruxelles ooh the drinks do not tamper with the word and can be appreciated without the finite loss of metaphor like the Andalusian girls under the Moorish wall to the whims of whores and whirls that wind there ways past the if fey and won't we have a merry time drinking whisky, beer, and wine at the James Joyce Irish Pub today.

Kafka's Café

Helsinki

Kafka never liked the insurance business. It brought in enough money, but he was always looking for other means to earn income and since he was clearly not interested in inheriting his father's business he was eager for investment opportunities. In his *"Conversations with Kafka"* Emil Janouch describes a particular encounter with Kafka when the latter told him about a short story on which he was working in which a man went to work only to discover all his co-workers were cockroaches. Janouch listened to the *maestro* explain the entire story before asking where he, Kafka, got the idea for such a macabré tale. Kafka responded that he went to his favorite café for his early morning coffee and as he walked into the kitchen (he always walked into the kitchen to "kibbitz with the cooks") all he could see was the chef, Gregor Samsa, attempting to kill scads of cockroaches swarming on the counter tops. "The sight disgusted me," said Kafka, "but I still kept going back there." The young Janouch asked why and Kafka responded, "The food is good and the place inspires me. Schmutzgeist."

Janouch told his father about the meeting and his father went to Kafka with the suggestion that they buy the café together and clean it up. Kafka was thrilled with the idea. With additional money invested by Max Brod, they purchased the café and began a search for a new, more original name. The Metamorphosis was suggested, but discarded; The Penal Colony, The Burrow, A Hunger Artist, The Next Village, and The Castle were all suggested, but all were discarded since they sounded too much "like titles for short stories or novels." Finally, exhausted from the task of trying to conceive a name, they decided simply on Kafka's Café.

The café was a major financial success and became a Prague institution. But after Kafka's death and the Nazi invasion, the café closed and it was only reopened after the thaw of Prague Spring in Los

Angeles where it's been a local hangout for movie moguls and wanna-be-screenwriters. Specializing in Giant Mole Burgers, Kafka's Café would make its namesake proud. As the footnote explains, the café was located on Melrose in West Hollywood across from the Cinegrill, but due to circumstances beyond Kafka's control, the café was subsequently moved from Hollywood to Helsinki.[21]

CHOCO LEIBNIZ™

Hannover

Everyone seems to think that only artists had trouble making ends meet in their quest to achieve the ends of their individual madness. Not so. Few know, for example, the true story behind what led to Leibniz's extraordinary philosophical theories. Five years after entering the University of Leipzig in 1666, at the ripe age of 15, Leibniz submitted a legal thesis for a doctoral degree. After lengthy deliberation, the committee rejected the thesis and the degree was denied. The rejection was clearly due to the tenderness of his age, not to the thoroughness of his thought, and Leibniz, distraught and fed up with legal studies, moved to Nuremberg to begin the study of alchemy and magic. It was there, at the age of 21, while tinkering in the kitchen of the Institute of Alchemical Solvents, that he stumbled upon the formula for what has since come to be known as the Choco Leibniz™. This discovery was not mercurial.

All his life, Leibniz struggled to reconcile the differences between the Romanists and Protestants, the Lutherans and Calvinists, in order to achieve harmony among *all* the religious groups in Germany. Except for the Jews, of course. The Choco Leibniz™, he felt, would no doubt achieve those ends, for Leibniz firmly believed that *there* was a cookie that every cookie-sucking German could agree on.[22] Alas, he was bitterly disappointed. None of the groups could agree on the relative amounts of the ingredients. The Romanists thought there was too much saturated fat (11 percent); the Protestants thought there was too little protein (2 percent); the Lutherans complained there wasn't enough dietary fiber (4 percent); and the Calvinists regarded a lack of Vitamins A and C to be sacrilegious. No one, of course, bothered to ask the Jews what they thought since their business was, well, too kosher.

Disappointed, Leibniz abandoned alchemical cookie-making and to the chagrin of many of his followers (who had dubbed him the

"Paracelsus of Pastry"), he once again returned to the study of philosophy. In 1676, he discovered the differential calculus which predated Newton's discovery by 17 years. Though Leibniz was bitterly disappointed about not being able to create a true "theodicy," he did discover through his baking experience, that each living organism, even those that delved into the cookie-baking process, had its own substantive form and that form was an essence of the nature of the soul. This discovery, also made at the Institute of Alchemical Solvents in Nuremberg, became the basis for his theory of monads and though he died in relative disgrace (since the English Newtonians, put off by the fact that Leibniz discovered the calculus before Newton [see "Fig Newtons™"], persuaded George I to deny Leibniz the Office of Royal Historiographer of England, but persuaded Newton to compete with Leibniz's cookies as well), he knew somehow that the recipe for Choco Leibniz™ would, some day, "make him some dough."

Defeated by George's rejection, Leibniz returned to Hannover, and though he was offered the position of Royal Baker, he knew his best cookie-baking days were over and he died unclarified and impecunious in 1716, but not before selling his cookie recipe to the Bahlsen family of Hannover, which has continued to maintain the integrity of the Choco Leibniz™. The philosopher would be happy knowing that today both Calvinists and Lutherans agree on that.

Fig Newtons™

East Hanover

Since both Leibniz and Newton were so unmitigatedly hostile towards each other, it would be sheer indifference indeed not to mention the origin of Fig Newtons™ after discussing the Choco Leibniz™. As was mentioned earlier, Newton and his followers were outraged with the fact that Leibniz had discovered the differential calculus almost two decades before the master. As one Newton biographer, Frank Manuel, put it, "Two of the greatest geniuses of the European world, not only of their own time, but of its whole long history, had been privately belaboring each other with injurious epithets and encouraging their partisans to publish scurrilous innuendoes in learned journals. In the age of reason, they [Leibniz and Newton] behaved like gladiators in a Roman circus." And even though both had discovered the calculus independent of each other, that span of time grated on Newton.

But their rivalry did not stop with the calculus. Nothing was beyond their criticism and as Manuel writes, their "views of all things in the heavens and on earth became polarized as they stalwartly assumed opposite positions, exaggerating their differences, grossly caricaturing each other's opinions like schoolboys in debate." This gnarly competition transcended philosophy to the much more rarefied climate of baking. Not to be outdone by Leibniz, especially on the cookie-baking front, Newton attended a number of baking workshops, trying to discover cookie dough that would challenge the legitimacy of the Choco Leibniz™. With Leibniz on his deathbed and Newton still having another decade to go, the latter spared nothing in an attempt to discover a cookie that would, more than anything else, decrease the amount of saturated fat.

One evening, while working diligently on yet another diatribe against Leibniz (this one concerning the former's refusal to abide by the fundamental principles of experimental baking [which were eventually published in the *Commercium epistolicum* (1714)] and to which Leibniz countered that any baking on Newton's part would merely result in "bad metaphysics"), he stumbled upon the idea for the perfect cookie to counter the Choco Leibniz™. It just so happens that while in the midst of writing the diatribe, Newton occasioned to overhear one of his fellow Newtonians arguing with a Leibnizian that not only was Leibniz a plagiarist, but that there wasn't a "fig of truth" in what he said. Actually, the Newtonian said, "sprig of truth," but just as Newton's apple was serendipitous, so too was Newton's fig.

It was at that moment Newton felt absolutely certain that such a fruit, if handled properly,[23] would have enormous commercial appeal if blanketed in the proper enriched wheat flour. He experimented with a number of different textures and designs before he came upon the Newton that we all recognize today. After weathering enormous problems in trying to patent the cookie (so the Leibnizians could not steal the idea) and spending enormous amounts of money, the Fig of Newton (which was its original Cambridge name) was first produced on 10 December 1716, the same day Leibniz died. The cookie was an immediate success and its reputation spread throughout Europe like wildfire, soon overtaking the popularity of the Choco Leibniz™ as "the cookie of champions."

Seeking a broader market, Newton sold the American rights to the Nabisco Corporation™, which paid Newton handsomely to produce the cookie and which garnered enough money for him to pay his patent attorneys and put something aside for his retirement. It also allowed Newton to entertain all the extravagances of his youth and to question all the curiosities. In the eternal truth of things, the Fig Newton™ has outsold the Choco Leibniz™, but in a kind of poignant irony, an irony that only Leibniz could possibly have appreciated, Nabisco™ bakes its Fig Newtons™ in Hanover. Should you wish to tour the company, Borges' Travel has special group rate discounts. Rental cars can be handled through Hemingway's Garage.

Poe's Cafeteria

Martinsville

"**O**h! Feckless strife torn asunder from the depth of my entrails, let me die with without so as not to render me totally impoverished," so Poe wrote in his still unpublished manuscript, *Grub Street in America* (1843) after garnering a paltry $52 for publication of his story "The Gold-Bug." This phase of Poe's life, generally referred to as the "Pheckless Philly Phase," was one of the most tragic, what with the fatal and futile combination of literary failure, gnawing poverty, and the terminal illness of his beloved wife, Virginia.

Those who knew him well recalled of Poe that "he walked the streets [of Philadelphia] in madness or melancholy, with lips moving in indistinct curses, or with eyes upturned in passionate prayer, or with his glances introverted to a heart gnawed with anguish and with a face shrouded in gloom." In short, Poe was not a happy camper in 1843. He was reduced to begging for money: five dollars here, ten dollars there. On one occasion, Poe took a copy of "The Raven" to William H. Graham, editor of *Graham's*, who flatly rejected it. In desperation he pleaded for his family's welfare, but Graham, staunch capitalist and advocate of what he called "supply-side economics"[24] was adamant; however, to further humiliate an already deeply humiliated man, Graham had Poe read the poem to the general staff, to which all of them, to a number, could only blink in bemusement at the constant refrain, "Nevermore."[25] Though the house consensus was to reject the piece, in deference to Poe's plight, the workers at the magazine passed the hat around and the beleaguered poet returned home with fifteen dollars.

It was on his way home, in the darkest of dark hours, that Poe, while rummaging through garbage to find something to eat, chanced upon a copy of the *Indianapolis Times* newspaper. What few people know is even in spite of Poe's sad state of affairs, the one thing that gave him succour was sport, and the sports he loved most were basketball and football. The discovery of the *Indianapolis Times* was serendipitous since his two favorite teams were the Indiana Hoosiers and the Indianapolis Colts, the latter of which's move from Baltimore prompted Poe's lugubrious novel *The Fall of the House of Irsay.* As Poe scanned the pages of the want ads he noticed one ad in particular:

Wanted
Part-time cashier
Martinsville Cafeteria
Good wages, clean work, free food

Now Martinsville, Indiana was a small town located a mere twelve miles from Bloomington (close to Indiana University) and only forty from Indianapolis (close to the Colts), so not only would such a job have allowed him the opportunity of eating, something which he had very little experience of, but also afforded him the luxury of following his two favorite teams.

Poe decided then and there that he and Virginia should move to Martinsville and begin a new life. He rushed back to Virginia. They packed in haste and took the first carriage to the Walnut Street Wharf from which they caught the Monon Rail to Indianapolis. This entire trip, which has gone virtually unnoticed by Poe scholars, was published in a little known work titled *Poe's Playbook,* edited with an introduction by the brilliant sports analyst, Branch McWooden. In it, McWooden states that the trip to Martinsville allowed Poe the freedom to write without worrying about the exigencies of eating, except during basketball and football season, when he made the Saturday journey to Bloomington and the Sunday journey to Indianapolis. But Virginia's continued poor health eventually forced him once again to move back to the east coast and after her death, his life, in ruins, was meager morsel for the festooned vultures that fed off him.

At his death, the restaurant owners, admirers of Poe's work,[26] though they didn't really understand it all, renamed the restaurant in his honor. It is not coincidental that the restaurant's specialty is *raven à la Poe.* The restaurant still flourishes and you can find one in Martinsville and another in Mooresville, Indiana.

Racine's Danish Kringles™

Racine

Poor Racine. Poor, poor Racine. Arguably France's greatest tragedian, Racine was born into a family of the upper bourgeoisie whose coat of arms was graced by a swan and a rat. Racine eventually dropped the rat, but "ratty" things certainly followed him throughout his life. Considered quite the ladies man, Racine finally settled down to marriage with Catherine de Romanet in 1677; however, the damage that Racine had done *vis-à-vis* his earlier indiscriminate trysts was to haunt him for a number of years thus, hurling him into rather precarious financial straits.

Though Racine was a well-known playwright in Paris, by the late 17th century drama itself wasn't very profitable for dramatists. Some things rarely change. But it is well-known that Racine had been able to furnish a house, collect rare books of some value, inherit money through his marriage, and by virtue of being made historiographer-royal (with Boileau), garner a salary of 2000 crowns. But even with that income, juggling finances was somewhat difficult. What really prompted Racine to consider alternative means of raising capital was the box-office failure of his play *Phèdre*. First staged at the Hôtel de Bourgogne in 1677, it was instantly met with an opposing *Phèdre* written by a rather obscure playwright by the name of Nicolas Pradon and was performed by the *troupe du roi*. The staging of the Pradon *Phèdre* was not serendipitous. It had been commissioned and supported by a number of Racine's detractors, including the Duchess of Bouillon and Madame Deshoulières, both of whom had amorous scores to settle with the writer of *Andromaque*. It seems that Racine's sexual dalliances were not taken so kindly by some of the more influential ladies of the nobility and they conspired to try to ruin him financially. As a matter of fact, Madame Deshoulières was quoted as saying about Racine that, "Il ne se prend pas pour une merde" or "he thinks highly of himself." There was invective from both sides, including some rather vitriolic reviews, but the end result was that the mediocre Pradon prevailed and Racine's *Phèdre* closed faster than David Letterman's version of *Hamlet*. Needless to say, Racine was distraught. When nothing could look worse, providence prevailed.

In a letter dated 18 January 1677, only weeks after the closure of his play, Racine was invited by his cousin, Jean-Baptiste Racine (for whom his eldest son was named), to come to America where he could "write in comfort next to the fresh water sea."[27] Jean-Baptiste was alluding to Lake Michigan, of course, since he and his family had founded the city of Racine, Wisconsin, some half-dozen years earlier. Given the chaos of Paris at the time, Racine leapt at the opportunity and sailed with his wife on 31 March 1677.

For the next four years, Racine remained in Racine not only writing the plays *Esther* and *Athalie*, but beginning what has since become known world-wide as the Racine Danish Kringle, the origins of which are quite remarkable. Prior to leaving France, Boileau, Racine's close friend and one who knew Racine's rather impecunious position, offered him a recipe for a Danish pastry which he had received from a Scottish sailor, who had received it from a British sea captain, who had received it from a Dutch shoemaker, who had received it from a Swedish fisherman, who had received it from a Norwegian farmer, who had received if from a Finnish dairyman, who had received it from a Danish prostitute. Or so Boileau said. Made from Wienerbrod dough, German apples, Alsace cherries, Brazilian nuts, Swiss chocolate, and buttercream icing, the pastry was "encroyable" according to Boileau,[28] who perceived that Racine could at least keep his family afloat by selling these "kringles," as they were called, in the new world. So he did and the rest has become Danish history. Or French.

Though Racine returned to France in 1681, Jean-Baptiste continued the business, which has remained in the family for over three centuries and which today mails kringles all over the world. Little do the eaters of what Boileau called "the biggest little secret in Europe" know that it was the kringle that inspired and sustained Racine while he was writing *Athalie*, possibly the finest of all French tragedies. One can still taste a bit of dramatic history, since the same kringle that sustained

Racine while writing some of the finest world literature can be ordered by contacting Racine Danish Kringles™ in Racine, Wisconsin. Their toll-free number is 1.800.4.DANISH. Tell them Racine sent you.

Café Strindberg

Helsinki

"What the fuck would you have me do, you fucking stupid idiotic bitch!" Those were the last words Strindberg allegedly spoke to his first wife, the Swedish actress Siri von Essen, in answer to her comment about "keeping his chin up" after the panning of his play *Creditors* in Stockholm, 1891. They divorced in 1891, shortly after the review came out. Always on the cusp of madness, Strindberg abandoned socialism for a kind of radical individualism which begat a religious conversion (1894-96) and his subsequent involvement in the mysticism of Emmanuel Swedenborg, an involvement which spawned a number of plays that met with disastrous results, including *Kabbalah Shuffle* (1894) and *The Fisher King* (1895), which was subsequently made into a film.

"What the fuck would you have me do, you fucking stupid idiotic bitch!" Those were the last words Strindberg allegedly spoke to his *second* wife, the Austrian journalist Frida Uhl, in answer to her comment about "keeping his chin up" after the panning of his play *Endzones of the Spirit* (1896). They divorced in 1896, shortly after the review came out. He began writing prose fiction after that time, including the little known trilogy of novels, *Whores* (1896), *Bitches* (1898), and *Cunts* (1900), all illustrated by Edvard Munch and all of which met with critical failure.

"What the fuck would you have me do, you fucking stupid idiotic bitch!" Those were the last words Strindberg allegedly spoke to his *third* wife, the Norwegian actress Harriet Basse, in answer to her comment about "keeping his chin up" after the review of his last novel alluded to it as "horribly misogynistic." They divorced in 1904, shortly after the review came out.

Totally frustrated and fatigued with the Swedish theatre-going public as well as the *literati*, he decided to take his money and move to Helsinki where he could do what he always wanted to do...open a café far enough away from the Swedish public (and women) that he could not "smell them."

Running Café Strindberg, he entertained poets, novelists, and playwrights alike, allowing them the freedom to perform as they desired, without fear of public humiliation and media reprisal. The café became a favorite respite for artists throughout Finland and Scandinavia: Sibelius drank there often and heavily, Dagerman and Søderberg read there, Hamsun sorted through the garbage there, and the café flourished long after Strindberg's death. But irony would not leave Strindberg alone. When he was on his deathbed, all his ex-wives, Siri, Frida, and Harriet, wrote him a collective letter with the news that he could run from the Swedish theatre but he could not hide since the new Svenska Theatre was going to be built right across the street from his café. The news caused him such convulsions it resulted in his immediate death. His last words were "cappuccino, please...fuck the women" (*Last Words of August Strindberg* 88). The café still remains on the Esplandi. Men are welcome; women are not.

Van Gogh's Potatoes

Turku

Realistically, what else could he do? Certainly selling paintings wasn't going to make him a living. Even a cursory reading of his *Letters to Theo* would attest to that. As an example, in a letter to his brother and sister dated 10 July 1890, van Gogh writes: "My money won't last me very long this time, for on my return I had to pay the bill for the luggage from Arles. I have some very good memories of that journey to Paris. A few months I hardly dared hoped to see my friends again. I think that Dutch lady (Saar de Swart) is most talented. Lautrec's picture, *Portrait de musicienne*, is quite wonderful, it moved me when I saw it." He also comments on another of Lautrec's paintings, *Portrait de sac à main*, which van Gogh laughed at, but which was a prescient sign at least for Lautrec (see "Lautrec's Handbags").

But given van Gogh's interest in things natural, in the earth, the soil, it was only fitting that with nothing to show for his work and the immediacy of his brother's finances always a question, van Gogh had to do something to make some money and potatoes were the answer.

In a subsequent letter to his mother, van Gogh writes that he was "absorbed in that immense plain with wheat fields up as far as the hills, big as the ocean, delicate yellow, delicate soft green, the delicate purple of a tilled and weeded piece of ground, with the regular speckle of the green of **flowering potato plants** (my bold) everything under a sky of delicate tones of blue, white, pink, and violet. I am in a mood of almost too much calm, just the mood needed for painting this." It was inevitable that van Gogh would do something to earn himself a living beyond his paintings, and his love of potatoes appeared to be his last salvation. In a letter to Theo dated 12 July, van Gogh says that he's been planting a particular kind of potato that would "bear the fruit of his soil and the flower of his life" and he seems optimistic that the potatoes would not only nurture his fascination for the natural things of the world, but would also bring in money for him to continue his art and to "pay for the contingencies of life."

Alas, things did not go well. A horrible drought in Provence proved disastrous for the plants and, inevitably, his spirit. In a letter dated 14 July, van Gogh repeats the simile of the horse and cart he used in an earlier letter, writing, "Disappointments—certainly, but we are no beginners & are like wagoners who by their horses' supreme efforts almost reach the top of the hill, do an about-turn, and then, often with one more push, manage to gain the top." Almost two weeks later, 29 July, van Gogh died in his brother's arms. Buried with many of his friends looking on—Bernard, Laval, Lucien Pissarro, Père Tanguy—van Gogh was laid to rest in the potato fields that were to nourish his art. The coffin was covered in yellow flowers. Though his effete venture into capitalism seemed to be a failure, potatoes grew on the site of his grave, tubers from which have been spread throughout the world. Farmers delight in van Gogh potatoes, swearing they are as sweet as they are indefatigable. Contrary to rumor, McDonald's™ does not use them, though they are used at Van Gogh's Brasserie, which is located in Amsterdam.

Virginia Woolf's Restaurant
London

What few people know is that *A Room of One's Own* was not only the name of Woolf's famous text (which came out of the Cambridge lectures she gave in the late 1920s), but also the name of a café located in the Russell Hotel, London. In those lectures, Woolf wittily and sarcastically expressed her dissatisfaction with the social and financial treatment women were receiving from men and felt the situation had to be remedied. It was out of those lectures that she came up with the idea of creating a venue for women to be able to congregate and share their ideas both as women and as writers.

On a beautiful spring day in 1930, Woolf invited Ethel Smyth, Rosamond Lehmann, Philippa Strachey, Victoria Sackville-West, and a number of other friends to Kew Gardens in order to discuss the possibilities of starting such a café. The possibility of creating such an eatery was greeted enthusiastically and the women organized themselves into committees to take care of each aspect of the restaurant: catering, advertising, marketing, etc. The biggest problem they confronted, of course, was one of finances: How to raise the money for such a café? In a letter dated 18 December 1930, Woolf writes to Ethel Smyth with the idea of selling the manuscript in order to raise money. She writes: "This is the usual scrawl, pending time to write at length (Thank God—off to Rodmell on Tuesday). And only to say, don't take any steps whatever, even imaginary, as yet about the MS of *Room*—I'm dealing cautiously with it and want to consult Philippa Strachey privately first." Unfortunately, nothing came of the meeting and they were still in difficulty in raising the funds.

As luck would have it, on the afternoon of 15 March 1931, while sitting in Kew Gardens, watching snails, thinking of marks on a wall, Woolf was approached by none other than E.M. Forster, who had only recently sold several of his novels to be made into films by

Merchant-Ivory. And even though Forster despised the cinema, he appreciated the cash. During their conversation, Woolf mentioned the idea of the café and the need to raise funds for it and Forster suggested she contact an independent film producer in the United States who was, he said, "always interested in the odd thing." One must remember that, at the time, Forster was not a major advocate of Woolf's work as any reading of *Aspects of the Novel* would show, yet, in good faith, Forster gave her the name of the producer, Raymond Krochleffel.[29]

Flushed with the possibility of finding a buyer for the manuscript, Woolf dashed off a letter to Krochleffel, who responded immediately by telegram with the succinct words: "I'll buy it." On 4 April 1931, Woolf and Krochleffel met in the foyer of the Russell Hotel. Papers were signed and a check was issued to Woolf for the manuscript. Woolf was thrilled, but unbeknownst to her, Krochleffel was a part owner in the hotel, a situation that would have significant implications later. Arrangements were made with the hotel to create *A Room of One's Own Café* at one entrance to the hotel, and the café opened for business on 1 May 1931, specializing in vegetarian foods, whole grains, and macrobiotic sandwiches. Leonard Woolf even cut the ribbon for the grand opening. The café was an enormous success and became *the* venue for women writers in London up to Woolf's death in 1941. Unfortunately, that's when the small print set in.

When Woolf signed the contract for the café, a clause in the contract stipulated that at the time of her death, the hotel reserved the right to change both the name of the café and the menu. There was no choice in the matter. Not long after her burial, the hotel immediately changed the name of the café to *Virginia Woolf's Restaurant* in order to capitalize on what Krochleffel said were the "obvious tourist possibilities." In addition, he took personal responsibility for changing from a vegetarian-based menu to a "burgers and pasta" menu which, he said, was something "tourists" would eat "quickly" since the object of the restaurant was not "loitering" but "turnover." Needless to say, he was right. The café slowly changed from a venue for women to share in the creative spirit to the fast-food debacle of Krochleffel's dreams. It continues to this day in the Russell Hotel, serving the same pasta and burgers that made Krochleffel a household name in the United States. And the manuscript which started it all, *A Room of One's Own*? Krochleffel sold it for a sizeable profit.

Café Voltaire

Ventura

What people fail to remember about Voltaire is that he became extremely wealthy, but the wealth came at no small price since it was as much a result of the acerbity of his tongue as it was of the art in his work. On more than one occasion, Voltaire was either soundly beaten or routinely jailed. Having been suspected of passing the words *Puero Regnante* and *J'aivu* as well as the ironic *Me ne fotto di soldi*, he was inveigled by a spy named Beauregard into a confession of some sort and was subsequently remanded to the Bastille in 1717. Several years later, after meeting Beauregard and insulting him, he was waylaid by him and, of course, beaten. Obviously, Voltaire's meager frame was too small to contain the size of his tongue which got him into trouble throughout his life. But many of those altercations were not necessarily a product of his sarcasm or his vitriolic anti-Semitism. Many of his quandaries were financially based since Voltaire was, above and beyond the literary artist, a financial scoundrel.

In 1751, he actually was accused of forgery. It was not an isolated case. Not only was he inordinately vain and patently anti-Semitic, he was totally unscrupulous in matters of money. Though his scathing texts like the *Diatribe du Docteur Akakia, Candide, L'Homme aux quarante écus* and *Zadig* are brilliant lampoons and polemics on religion, philosophy, etc., rarely did he engage in lampooning his own greed.

The dramatic upshot of all this economic *Sturm und Drang* was that by 1754 he was *persona non grata* in France. He moved to Switzerland and bought a country house which he named *Les Délices* that bordered the canton Vand. But he bought other houses as well so as not to be without refuge in case, as he was once quoted as saying, "his tongue got his ass in trouble." It was during his trip to England (1726-29) where he met, among others, Bolingbroke, Congreve, Pope, the Walpoles and, from the United States, Moxley Turnbull, a world-class surfer and first winner of the Duke Kahanamoku surfing competition in Hawaii. It was Turnbull who suggested to Voltaire that he think about buying property in America, specifically on the west coast. In case things in Europe got "too hot," Moxley suggested, "you could chill out on the coast."

The advice was heeded and on his one and only trip to America for the production of *Zaïre,* at the Ventura County Playhouse (1776), Voltaire purchased some property in the city of Ventura. On his death, the property converted to his adopted daughter Reine Philiberte de Varicourt and her husband, the Marquis de Villette. The two visited Ventura in 1785 after purchasing some land in Carmel and opened a café which, at the time, only catered to wayward poets, slackers, and surfers, but over time it has become known up and down the coast for its *"Voltaire Jolt,"* a mixture of espresso, ice cream, milk, chocolate syrup, and coffee grinds accompanied by not one, but two Choco Leibnizes™! Nothing would have made Voltaire prouder.

Part II
Of Fashion, Flowers, & Accessories

Bukowski Jewelers

Helsinki

What prompted Bukowski to give up writing and open a jewelry store is one of the most fascinating stories in contemporary fiction. Who would have thought that someone so ingrained with the plight of the marginal members of American society would, ultimately, abandon them in favor of selling high-priced jewelry? But like everything else about Bukowski, this apparent "sell-out" was merely that: apparent.

Certainly Bukowski's "fucking, fighting, and philandering" only prepared him for the vicissitudes of fiction. One need only read *Erections, Ejaculations, Exhibitions and General Tales of Ordinary Madness* to get a sense of where Bukowski/Chinaski had been and where Bukowski/Chinaski was going. But the real genius behind Bukowski's investment in jewelry starts with the writing of the screenplay *Bar Fly* (1987)—starring Mickey Rourke—and his subsequent novel *Hollywood* (1989). In the novel, a tax accountant tells Chinaski to spend the advance money he got for writing a screenplay before the government takes it.

Curiously, Bukowski was in the same situation as Chinaski. In a chapter not included in the novel, but in the original manuscript, Chinaski has dinner with Bukowski at Spago. The two discuss what they should do with the money that Bukowski has made from the film *Bar Fly* as well as the advance money Chinaski made from his own script. Needless to say, as any discussion with Bukowski might, the discussion became heated, heated to the point that Bukowski threatened Chinaski with his life if he didn't "come up with a fucking good idea!"[30] Chinaski, of course, wasn't going to take "any shit" from Bukowski and told him "shut your fucking mouth, or I'll shut it for you!" Bukowski had to make a decision at this point whether to get rid of Chinaski or to write himself out of the novel. This was a difficult decision to make. Caught between the violent contradictions of postmodernity and whatever the contradiction of that might be, Bukowski did the next best thing: he asked the waitress, Darla.

Darla, who was certainly floozier than anyone Bukowski had ever written about before, merely opined, "Diamonds are a girl's best friend." Genius indeed! Bukowski had his answer: invest the money in the jewelry business as a tax advantage and a hedge against inflation.

And so he did, but Bukowski was not one to forget his roots. Beyond all the scatological elements in Bukowski's life and work, there was a deeply seeded fondness for the marginals in society, for the downtrodden, the outcasts, the voiceless ones. So the jewelry store was merely a pretext for something more important for Bukowski and the money he made from the store was contributed to the Meat School Soup Kitchen for the homeless, the hopeless, and other poets.

Céline Leathers

Buenos Aires

C ould there have been any doubt, as one journeys to the end of the night, paying death on the installment plan, that Céline (born Louis-Ferdinand Destouches) would have gone into the leather business? None at all, especially given his remarkable relations with the Nazis. One merely needs to read in *L'Ecole des cadavres:* "Who is the true friend of the people? Fascism is. Who has done the most for the working man? The USSR or Hitler? Hitler has.... Who has done the most for the small businessman? Not Thorez but Hitler!" And it's true.

Though it is widely known that Céline was a practicing obstetrician, it is a little known fact that he eventually opened a leather goods store in order to raise money to make a film version of his *Voyage au bout de la nuit*. At first, he had anticipated securing Hollywood financing for such a venture, but being completely ignorant about the money involved in Hollywood filmmaking (this was a problem for Brecht as well), not to mention what Hollywood *would* film, he failed. Rather than accept the obvious fact that *Voyage* was not a "Hollywood film commodity," and that one didn't have to be Louis B. Mayer to figure that out, Céline railed against Hollywood and American movies as being manifestations of a decadent Jewish culture. Declaring the film and publishing businesses were run by "slimy Jews who have no appreciation of art" (*Bagatelles pour un massacre* 107) (a curious comment since it was a "slimy Jew," Bernard Steele, who helped get Céline's novel *Hôtel du Nord* published) he returned to Paris in 1936 to raise the money himself.

During the course of trying to borrow money, Céline applied to a number of "Jewish banks" run by men like Rothschild, Lazare, and Baruch, but he was turned down by all of them simply because his financial prospectus was, quite frankly, unreadable. Outraged at his inability to write a readable prospectus he once again turned his invective against Jews, claiming that the "Jew and Freemason dog tear away a few new goodies each day, cadaverous snatches; they stuff them-selves, what a blow-out! thrive on them, gloat, exult, they go delirious on carrion" (*Je l'emmerde* 173). An ironic statement indeed since he eventually got into the "carrion" business himself.

Rejected by the "Jew kike corn-holers," he turned to the Paris branch of the NSBA (the Nazi Small Business Administration) for a loan to assist him in beginning his business, a business which was, of course, ideal, since he knew he could get "skins" at well below whole-sale costs from his Polish, Vichy, and Bavarian distributors, and his connections with those in the medical field would pay off more than handsomely. At first, Céline had thought about going into the soap business, perfumed soaps actually, but felt there wasn't enough margin to make it as profitable as the "skins game."

The Nazis cordially lent him the money at an extremely attractive interest rate, and Céline, filled with renewed enthusiasm, not to men-tion devoted gratitude to both the Führer and Friedmanian econom-ics, conducted a demographic survey to see what his market might be. However, his overt racism cut into what potential markets there might have been since, he said, "the Jews, Afro-Asiatic hybrids, quadroons, half-negroes, and Near-Easterners, unbridled fornicators, have no rea-son to be in this country" (*Va te faire enculer* 69).[31]

Unfortunately, that sales approach was not in the best interest of the company and after minimal financial success (the business did not raise the necessary capital to film *Voyage*) and Céline's eventual impris-onment (he was convicted of conducting acts detrimental to the national defense and of furthering the designs of the Axis powers), he was forced to liquidate the company to a Herr J. Koenigsburg[32] who, using the Céline name, reopened the store in Buenos Aires before franchising the shops throughout South America, where they success-fully operate today.

Dujardin Children's Clothes

Brussels

L iterary fame had always eluded Dujardin. The novel he wrote in 1887, *Les lauriers sont coupés (We'll to the Woods No More)*, was quickly dismissed after its publication. It appeared serially in 1887, was recognized by Dujardin's friend, George Moore, as something worthy to read, and was soon forgotten. But the work itself was, of course, "cutting-edge" fiction, since Dujardin had created the *interior monologue,* which Joyce read in 1902 and which he subsequently acknowledged as the major source for *Ulysses.*[33]

With the blessings of the high priest of modernism, Dujardin struck out with a new career: a lecturer, lecturing on something he wrote, but didn't quite understand himself, that is to say, interior monologue. His invitations to Germany, Italy, and Belgium all ended rather disastrously and as Joyce's influence and reputation grew, Dujardin's did not. Dissatisfied with the direction of his career, he gave up writing altogether, but unlike Rimbaud, Dujardin had no interest in pursuing a career in arms sales.

Enter George Moore. Moore, an Irish writer, was deeply into café society in Paris and was a close friend of Dujardin's. Though a dandy like Dujardin in *fin de siècle* Paris, Moore also had a kind of "naturalistic" streak in him that allowed him to think of more practical matters; certainly it was a practical matter that prompted him to give up the café life and return to Ireland to manage his estate. While sitting with Dujardin at the Rotonde, trying to lighten Dujardin's "creative spirits," Moore suggested Dujardin take another path, start a new career, fashion design, for example. He reminded Dujardin that writing wasn't everything, that even Rimbaud gave it up for rifles and Hemingway for garages, so why not Dujardin?

But nothing seemed to help Dujardin, who was utterly lost in his own self-pity when, at that very moment, an unattended baby carriage came hurtling down a staircase before hitting the pavement. Moore saw the frantic mother trying to chase down the stroller, but the quick-thinking Dujardin immediately ran after the carriage and grabbed it seconds before it and the toddler within would have tumbled tragically over the curb. The mother was none other than Françoise Verhaeren, Emile Verhaeren's youngest sister, who was visiting Paris from Brussels and who was eternally grateful to Dujardin for saving her son's life. It was serendipitous that Françoise mentioned the reason she traveled to Paris was to buy clothes for her son. Dujardin asked why that was so and Verhaeren mentioned there was nothing in Brussels. As I said, Dujardin was and had always considered himself a dandy, and attire was as important to him as fine wax on a curled mustache. One thing led to another and Moore suggested that both Dujardin and Verhaeren open a children's clothing store in Brussels. With the Verhaeren name and Dujardin's taste in clothing, it seemed like a perfect match.

On 31 March 1905, Dujardin Children's Clothes opened for business with Emile Verhaeren cutting the ribbon and writing a poem for the store, which was included in his collection *Les Heures d'apres-midi* (1905). The store resides today at 82-84 Avenue Louise, Brussels, and with every purchase over sixty dollars one receives a free copy of *Les Lauriers sont coupés*.

Kipling Camping Gear™

Cambridge

It should be no more surprising than Borges' Travel, should it? One has only to look at the surfeit of stories, of animal fantasy stories, to realize that any monetary investment Kipling might have made would go into something like camping equipment or rucksacks or some other accoutrement that would take one on a walk into nature. It was the publication of *A Walking Delegate*, by consensus one of Kipling's least tolerable animal stories, that really initiated the idea.

Kipling had long been accused of being a Fascist by contemporaries like Orwell and Lewis. If his notions on how "superior" men should treat "inferior" men reached their penultimate artistic conclusions with *Captains Courageous*, then they reached their penultimate social conclusions with *A Walking Delegate*. Certainly Kipling's kind of glorified social cleansing may have pleased General Patton, but most reactions to the book were quick and vitriolic. Already hostile to the press as early as 1891, Kipling said to intrusive journalists upon leaving the United States, "Well, you won't have Kipling to kick around anymore."[34]

Kipling was always interested in "men of action" and as such preferred a kind of rugged, autocratic individualism that was cut in men like Rhodes and Roosevelt, which made them models for Kipling's veneration. Needless to say, Kipling had a personal attachment to both these men and the letters between Roosevelt and Kipling are fascinating for their insights into the war and European history and culture. But it is the letter that Roosevelt wrote to Kipling in December, 1934, that gives a key to what Kipling eventually did. In that letter, Roosevelt suggests to Kipling that he consider "investing in the outdoors" as a way to get in touch with his "inner animal."[35]

Kipling never forgot those words and subsequent to the horrible reviews of *A Walking Delegate*, Kipling decided to abandon writing altogether and with his wife Caroline, who had helped him triumph over financial disaster in the past, invested some money in a rucksack store in Cambridge. Little did he know the little rucksack shop in Cambridge would become more well-known than the author who inspired it.

Lautrec Handbags

Brussels

Toulouse-Lautrec spent a lot of time in brothels, sketching subjects whom he admired, while making no distinction as to their social status. His sketch *Woman Fixing Her Stocking* (1894) or *La Visite: Rue des Moulins* (1894) would attest to that. Such an approach to painting his subjects was not uncommon for Lautrec. What was rather uncommon was that he would often receive friends, associates, and creditors in the same brothels. These meetings were a bit disconcerting, specifically for his creditors, some of whom were clients of the same subjects that Lautrec was painting. One such visitor to the brothel was a M. Henri Menottes, whom the prostitutes affectionately called "être à court de d'argent" for the obvious reason that Menottes was constantly trying to bargain with the prostitutes for their services. An investment banker, Menottes knew a good deal when he found one and would only pay according to what he thought the service was worth. As a matter of fact, it's a well-known fact among Parisian prostitutes even today that it was Menottes who coined the Duchamps phrase "This is not a pipe" when one was not entirely satisfied with a job.

At any rate, it was Menottes who was one of Lautrec's biggest patrons and had long been fascinated with the "petit queue" as he called him, and his paintings of women. Between 1892-1896, Menottes had purchased such paintings as *La Goulue Entering the Moulin Rouge* (1892), *La Visite* (1894), *Chilperic* (1896), among others, and was fascinated with Lautrec's sense of the ironic, but always wondered why he never included handbags in any of his paintings of women. After one particular "jouissance," Menottes actually asked Lautrec the question, but the painter merely hinted that as much as he liked them they tended to "clutter the composition" and the conversation stopped there.

But in a letter dated 4 August 1896, Menottes, who could be a very generous man and who was well aware of Lautrec's physical limitations, wrote to him with the suggestion that he consider "going into business" as a "hedge against old age," especially when the "glimmer of soiled lives lost its sheen."[36]

At Menottes' request, they met and Menottes arranged the financing for the business. Lautrec was thrilled with the possibility of incorporating handbags into his paintings and of having a business that would eventually make him financially solvent. The store opened for business in Paris on 5 October 1896 and was extremely successful. When Lautrec died in 1901, Menottes, who grieved terribly, kept the store open under Lautrec's name. It was taken over by Menottes' family, moved to Brussels (where they added a line of Verlaine and Villon shoes and Evita hosiery) and run by them as late as 1999 when, ironically, the last of the Menottes had decided to close the business because he wanted to "become a painter."

Monet Jewelry™

New York

Given the current rate for an original Monet, no one would have imagined the master was a beggar for most of his adult life. But the fact he actually sold his paintings door-to-door and that he constantly pleaded for loans is clearly established in his correspondence. An example of such impecunity is found in a letter sent to Renoir's patron, publisher Georges Charpentier, in which Monet writes: "For ten days I have been in Paris without being able to find a penny and I am unable to return to the country where my wife is so ill. You would render me a great service in giving this sum (5-6 louis) to the bearer and as soon as I have returned definitely to Paris I will come see you and reimburse you either in paintings or in money" (*Correspondence* 274).

So, you see, he was often (if not totally) in financial straits. But after he was evicted by Mme. Aubry-Vitet from her country house in Argenteuil and before Zola refused him a loan, Monet came up with a fascinating scheme.

The idea occurred to him shortly before Christmas, 1877, and just after Manet had visited the despondent Monet in his rundown Paris *atelier.* Of this meeting we also know from a letter Manet wrote to his friend Théodore Duret on Monet's behalf. Manet wrote: "I went to see Monet yesterday. I found him quite broken down and in despair. He asked me to find someone who will take ten or twenty of his pictures at 10 francs each, the purchaser to choose which he liked. Shall we arrange the matter between us, say 500 francs each? Of course no one, he least of all, must know that the offer came from us." In a postscript, Manet wrote: "As a gift, I left Camille a pair of gold earrings I had discovered in Clignacourt. It warmed her day" (*Correspondence* 286).

It was the gift that stirred Monet since, he drew a connection among Manet, the giver; Camille, the receiver; and the earrings, the gift. And suddenly the idea of direct-mail marketing occurred to him.

"Why should people go to stores to shop for jewelry?" Monet wrote to Manet in a letter dated 25 December 1877. "Why not bring jewelry to the people!" Manet was fascinated by the idea.

With Monet doing the ad designs, Zola writing the copy, Camille Claudel designing the jewelry, and Manet handling the finances and marketing, Monet Jewelry made its debut on 1 January 1878. The direct mail business was an extraordinary success in Paris and it was only a short time later that the marketing idea spread throughout France and Europe.

After Monet's death, his son Jean took over the business and broadened the marketing area to include both South and North America and today, Monet Jewelry™, sold by major department stores like Dayton's™ and Robinsons-May™, does an extraordinary business. Little did Monet know, contemplating suicide, and starving in that Paris garret with a sick and pregnant wife and a malnourished child, that such an idea, born in poverty, would become a multimillion dollar business, far outstripping the money he could have made merely as a painter. Today the reflection of those halcyon days in Giverney is seen in the beauty that endures in a Monet Pearl™.

Evita Perón Hosiery

Buenos Aires

There was no better place than Buenos Aires for an aspiring actress in the 1930s. The city was filled with theaters willing to give talented actors a chance at the big time. Unfortunately, Evita was not very talented nor did she have any theatrical training. Couple that with the fact she dressed poorly and had a provincial accent, Evita had no chance of becoming an actress, though she was given a great opportunity to suffer, as an interview with a fellow actor friend Pierina Dealessi indicates: "She looked so thin and delicate that I used to add a little milk to her maté to give her some nourishment. She weighed nothing at all. What with hunger, poverty, want, and general neglect, her hands were always cold and damp.... She had a beautiful bust, but it hung badly because she was so skinny. She once borrowed my stockings to build it up a bit—poor kid."

Evita's persistence finally paid off when she began doing broadcasts of soap operas on Radio Belgrano. It was through that job that she became the mistress of Colonel Anibal Imbert and it was through him that she finally met Juan Perón. We all know what happened after that, but what few people know is that Evita Perón had an obsession. Now this obsession wasn't like Verlaine's obsession with shoes, but it was very similar, for she was always remembered as "the girl with borrowed stockings," a nickname that haunted her for most of her adult life.

Determined to overcome that odious moniker, Evita convinced Perón to allow her to create a line of socks called Evita Perón Hosiery. At first, Perón thought it "stupid" and we know that fact from Evita's book *La Razon de mi Vida*. But we also know she finally convinced El Juan when she said, "I envision a line of hosiery that will be erotic from foot to waist, in white and black lace, embroidered only in those places where imagination rules" (*La Razon de mi Vida* 75). Perón needed a tablecloth to wipe his mouth. Evita got the money and created the line, which spread from Argentina to Italy. So successful was the line that it continues to this day, operated by Evita's Secrete, a lingerie company with offices in Paris, Sydney, Buenos Aires, and Temuco.

Evita's Socks can be purchased in fashionable stores worldwide, including Harrods of London.

Ravel Shoes™

Paris

It should be obvious to anyone who knows Ravel's life that the influence of his Basque mother, Marie Delouart, was considerable. Ravel has written that some of his earliest childhood memories were of the Spanish lullabies his mother would sing to him at night and through her he gained an interest not only in the Basque country, but the people and music of Spain. What most people don't know is that his mother also introduced him to something else that was uniquely Spanish: shoes.

In a letter written by Manuel de Falla, commenting on Ravel's *Rapsodie espagnole,* he writes: "The rhapsody surprised me by its Spanish character.... But how could I explain the subtly authentic Hispanic quality of our musician, knowing, by his own admission, that he had but neighboring relations with our country, being born near its frontier? I rapidly solved the problem: Ravel's Spain was a Spain ideally presented by his mother, whose refined conversation, always in excellent Spanish, delighted me, particularly when she would recall her youthful years spent in Madrid and her complete fascination for fashionable shoes."[37]

But it wasn't until many years later that Ravel would turn that motherly fascination of leather into something more tangible. The origins of Ravel Shoes™ really began after the success of *Boléro,* which was introduced at the Paris Opéra by Madame Rubinstein in November, 1928. Its popularity spread rapidly. In January, 1930, Ravel recorded it with the Lamoureux Orchestra; subsequently, Toscanini and the New York Philharmonic led a performance of the work at the Paris Opéra and by 1934, Paramount released a film titled *Boléro,* starring Carole Lombard and George Raft. Not only did *Boléro* become his most widely known composition, but it was the making of the film and the subsequent meeting of Carole Lombard that initiated the entire shoe business.

As serendipity would have it, Ravel met Lombard on the set of the film while she was dressing. Ravel, whose foot fetish wasn't nearly as obsessive as either Verlaine's or Villon's, still liked to gaze at a good pair of leather shoes. When Lombard walked out, Ravel was mesmerized by the glistening pair of black, white, and brown leather spiked heels and immediately stopped her to ask where she purchased them. Lombard said she couldn't remember, but it was a store she had visited in Barcelona. The two began chatting about their mutual love of shoes when Clark Gable, Lombard's husband at the time, was asked by Ravel what interest he had in shoes. Bored with the idle chatter, he was to have merely sputtered, "Frankly, Maurice, I don't give a damn...but maybe the two of you should open a store together." The idea fascinated both of them and after negotiating the possibilities of such, a store was opened next to the Montmartre restaurant *Auberge de la bonne franquette*, a location selected because of the high volume of artistic notables who frequented the eatery. The store now has a worldwide franchise following, specializing, of course, in *Boléro Boots*,[38] the mainstay of the store's stock.

RODIN'S LADIES APPAREL™

Paris

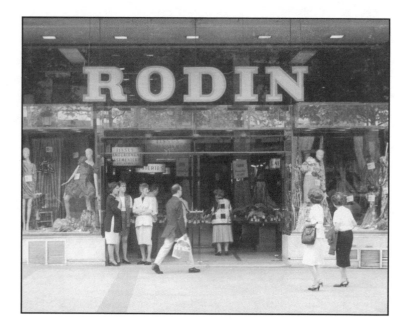

R odin was not in need of money. Camille Claudel was. Hence, the rather remarkable story of the genesis of this business. It is common knowledge that Claudel was Rodin's mistress. What isn't of common knowledge is the influence that Rilke, who was then Rodin's secretary, was to have on Rodin's decision to begin the business.

Rodin had so much money that in 1908 Rilke suggested to Rodin that he purchase the Hôtel Biron as a place to live and work, but the latter postponed buying the property in hopes the state would purchase it as a museum for his work, which it did. The entire hotel episode is an example of how influential Rilke was in Rodin's life and how financially secure Rodin actually was. It is also a well-known fact that Rodin loved women. Lots of women. Claudel was only one. His chaotic relationship with the Duchesse de Choiseul is well-documented as is his long-time marriage to Rose Beuret. But his relationship with Claudel has only recently been a matter of investigation. Some light has been shed on their relationship and, specifically, on the business they began through an obscure pamphlet published by Rilke himself the same year Rodin died, 1917.[39]

In the pamphlet, Rilke recounts a breakfast he had with Rodin in which *the maestro* told him of a strange "vision" he had seen in a dream. The vision, according to Rilke, was the origin for the *Balzac* statue with the one difference being that it was Camille Claudel beneath the robe and not Balzac. Rodin asked Rilke what he thought that meant, to which the novice answered that, perhaps, it was a kind of transfiguration in which he, Rodin, felt that Claudel was worthy of more than the minimal kind of recognition he had given her. That perception was truly the case, because Rodin rarely gave Claudel the kind of accolades she deserved as a fellow artist nor did she ever get much money from him on which to survive. "But what of the cloak?" Rodin was to have asked, dismissing the implication that he didn't really give her the respect she was due. Rilke writes that he thought it, the robe, had something to do with Claudel's interest in fashion. After all, while Duncan resided at the Hôtel Biron, Claudel visited her repeatedly and was even seen wearing Duncan's dresses at parties and late-night soirées. "But she cannot afford those kind of dresses," Rodin was to have said. Exactly, Rilke writes, and perhaps that's what the dream was telling him. "To do what?" Rodin asked. Perhaps, to open a dress shop for her. Rodin was convinced by Rilke's answer.

According to Rilke, Rodin purchased a building on the Champs-Élyssès and opened the store called Rodin, apparel for women. One may be wondering why, if it were a store for Claudel, it wouldn't have been called Claudel or Camille. The answer rests in Rodin's marketing savvy. Rodin was as shrewd a businessman as he was a sculptor and he felt that since no one in Paris really knew who Claudel was, only his name would bring in customers and establish a devoted clientele, thereby securing financial success for the store and, ultimately, for Claudel herself. The store was decorated, the stock was purchased, and then, as a surprise, on 31 March 1898, days after the *Monument to Balzac* was exhibited, Rodin brought Claudel to the store, blindfolded.

According to Rilke, when Rodin removed the blindfold, Claudel was to have said after blinking at the sign, "What is it?" Rodin answered, "Your store." "Then why does it have *your* name?" she asked. "Because," he said, "no one knows yours." According to Rilke, Claudel then slapped Rodin across the face and said, "Je m'en fous et m'en contrefous!" and stormed off. Nonplussed, since there was an enormous crowd in attendance, Rodin apparently shrugged it off and, with Rilke in tow, rushed into the store to celebrate its opening before returning to his *atelier* to continue his work-in-progress, *The Gates of Hell.*

The store is still owned by the Rodin family though, curiously, it is managed by Claudel Enterprises, a division of Pittsburgh Paint and Glass™.

Söderberg's Florists

Minneapolis

It is widely accepted that the famous Swedish writer Hjalmar Söderberg was greatly influenced in his shorter writings by both de Maupassant and Anatole France, but his genius lay in his tiny masterpiece, *Dr. Glas* (1905), a small work which raises the moral question: Is it right to take the life of a useless or dangerous human being? The lonely physician in the story becomes a murderer in order to free a young woman from her husband, an unsympathetic clergyman; however, the wife is abandoned by her new lover and in the midst of the horror a sharp, ironic light is cast upon the doctor and his attempt to remedy the arbitrariness of life. This arbitrariness was to haunt Söderberg throughout his own life and it wasn't until he gave up writing for the floral business that he could be at peace with it.

Though Söderberg loved Stockholm, the smell of the city and the city life, its Bohemian cafés and his life as a *flâneur*, it was his growing marital difficulties that forced him to leave Stockholm for Copenhagen, where he lived a kind of self-imposed exile. Söderberg had a keen eye for the weaknesses of humankind and most of his works were marked by a mixture of laconic irony and a deep sense of the tragic. Curiously, most of his major work was written prior to the time he left Stockholm, and when he got to Denmark he began to write more spiritual and philosophical works, such as *Jesus Barabbas* (1928) and *Den förvandlade Messias* (*The Transformed Messiah,* 1932).

It was also at that time, in the early 1930s, that Söderberg wrote scathing articles which were highly critical of Fascist and Nazi thought and the regimes that professed them. But the ensuing horrors of the Nazi occupation tended to debilitate his senses and eventually led to a complete loss of interest in the meaning of writing. So what does a socially conscious writer do when weariness and emptiness weighs so heavily upon the senses? When the bleakness of the

Scandinavian landscape is only intensified by the bleakness of the inhumanity of man? Flowers.

It was on an autumn day in 1933, shortly after *The Transformed Messiah* was published in Denmark, that Söderberg had a chance meeting with Hans Christian Andersen. Now the two of them had known each other through their respective works, but they had never actually met until they were invited to a party given by Axel Käpp, yet another writer who, like Söderberg, was a student of the Scandinavian *fin-de-siècle* school of humanistic pessimism. Käpp was a highly opinionated Jewish novelist famous for his ironic novels and scathing wit, who had lived in Denmark all his life and who was high on the Nazi "hit list" because he had written "disparaging remarks about the Führer's sexual preferences."[40] Käpp had close ties with many German writers, including Alfred Döblin, and he knew exactly what Jewish horrors were transpiring in the minds of the Nazis as early as 1933. But it was Andersen who, upon hearing about Söderberg's depression, told him a story about a friend of his who, after opening a flower shop, had discovered it altered his life. "Nothing was quite the same after that," Andersen told Söderberg. "His entire world-view had changed. The role of nature in the universe, the role of man in nature, the role of God in man, were all resplendent ideas seen in the variegations of a leaf or in the petals of a flower." Söderberg didn't need much convincing and soon thereafter opened a flower shop on Frederiksberg Allé (presently the home of the internationally known film director, Henning Carlsen) and began the life of a florist.

Indeed, Andersen could not have been more right. Everything was progressing grandly for Söderberg until the Nazi invasion of Denmark and upon hearing of Käpp's execution by the Gestapo (a most violent and grotesque death), Söderberg could neither arrange sentences nor carnations and felt compelled to escape the continent. But to where? Then he recalled a meeting he once had with Knut Hamsun (long before Hamsun's own Nazi affiliations) about America, specifically the Midwest of America, and Minneapolis in particular. He recalled that Hamsun, though not very complimentary about Chicago, had gentle praise for Minneapolis and its natives as a place of "warm and compassionate people, as tolerant and progressive as their winters were long" (*Hamsun in America* 115).

With little reluctance (and with Andersen's financial assistance), Söderberg crammed all of his belongings into the backseat of his Saab and sailed from Copenhagen to New York, from where he drove to Minneapolis where, without the threat of Nazi persecution, he opened a new flower shop on Lake Street just across the river from St. Paul. It's a flower shop that specializes in the Butterfly Pea, an homage to his friend Axel Käpp. The flower shop thrives to this day.[41]

Verlaine Shoes

Paris

While attending the famous Lavender Influences in Psychoanalytic Studies Convention (1899), a gay and lesbian psychoanalytic convention, Freud commented that it was Verlaine's poetry which actually prompted him to write his seminal paper on "fetishism" in the *Three Essays* (1905). It was, in fact, Verlaine's poem "Les chasseurs et la femme" (1867) [from the lesbian collection of sonnets titled *Les Amies*] that prompted Freud, as a follow-up to his study on da Vinci, to write: "When now I announce that the fetish is a substitute for the penis, I shall certainly create disappointment; so I hasten to add that it is not a substitute for any chance penis, but for a particular and quite special penis that had been extremely important in childhood but had later been lost. That is to say, it should normally have been given up, but the fetish is precisely designed to preserve it from extinction. To put it more plainly: the fetish is a substitute for the woman's (the mother's) penis that the little boy once believed in and— for reasons familiar to us—does not want to give up." After reading Verlaine's poem, Freud went on to write: "Thus the foot or shoe owes its preference as a fetish to the circumstance that the inquisitive boy peered at the woman's genitals from below, from her legs up; fur and velvet—as has long been suspected—are a fixation of the sight of pubic hair, which should have been followed by the longed-for-sight of the female member." It's certainly clear from such poems as "A Une Femme" or "Ballade Sappho" or 'Beauté des femmes, leur faibless" or "La Belle au Bois dormait" and from Verlaine's erotic poetry, that Verlaine's decision to open a woman's shoe store based on this fetish was inevitable. Not only is that obvious in the poem, "Les chasseurs et la femme," but in his correspondence with Rimbaud. In a letter dated as early as August, 1873 (while Verlaine was incarcerated for shooting Rimbaud), Rimbaud mentions to Verlaine that he "might be better off

opening a women's shoe store. Somewhere on the Champs (sic)"
(*Rimbaud Correspondence* 175).

Almost twenty years later (1890), when Rimbaud was looking for
business opportunities in which to invest some of the money he made
from the sale of guns in Abyssinia, the idea had not diminished. Not
only did Rimbaud invest in Verlaine's shoe store, but, with Verlaine as
regional manager, actually opened his own shoe store in Marseilles in
1891, two years before he died. Actually, Verlaine became so absorbed
with things female, he considered a sex change operation as late as
1894. Dissuaded by Rimbaud to undertake the surgery, he took up
cross-dressing instead and was buried in the same skirt and heels he
had designed for Coco Chanel. The store, located next to a thriving
McDonald's™ on the Champs Élyssès, is still one of the most fashionable in Paris.

FRANÇOIS VILLON SHOES

Paris

Prior to 1997, one could only speculate on the origin of Verlaine's perfervid interest in women's shoes (see Verlaine Shoes). But the latest publication of an incredible text discovered in the cloister of the University church of St. Benoît-le-Bientourné on the Rue St. Jacques and re-published by Flammarion, not only sheds startling light on the possible origins of Verlaine's fetish, but also answers heretofore unanswerable questions about Villon's life after his disappearance in 1463. The book, simply titled *Jangleresse* and written by an anonymous writer, addresses Villon's relationship with the Coquillards who were composed of "the best card-sharpers, brigands, footpads, dice-coggers, crimps, Mohocks, mumpers, pimps, ponces, horse-stealers, confidence-men, bruisers, thugs, lock-pickers, coin-clippers, housebreakers, hired assassins, and all-round desperadoes in Europe"[42] and also attests to the fact that Villon's *Ballade to Our Lady* is nothing more than a paean to his interest in women's shoes and that his disappearance was nothing of the kind, but a way for him to restart his life after the death of the priest Philip Chermoye[43]—with whom Villon had a long-standing feud—and his imprisonment at Meun-sur-Loire on charges stemming from a minor theft. The author attests that the poem actually relates to a woman Villon seduced, a prostitute, who had such glorious feet that he raised the woman and her feet to ethereal heights. Hence the phrase "n'avoir les cieulx, je n'en suis jangleresse," which accounts for both the woman's celestial significance and Villon's incorrigibility.

And though the woman, whose name has been lost to history, was the driving force behind Villon's interest in shoes, it was only at Meun-sur-Loire in 1461 that his interest in designing women's shoes grew since part of his rehabilitation was to design leather lasts for women's shoes. Subsequent to his release in 1462, Villon returned to Paris where he met François Ferrebourg, or Ferrebouc, a priest, Bachelor of Arts, Licentiate in Canon Law, Pontifical Notary, and Writer to the Officiality of the Bishop of Paris. He was also very interested in going into business and, upon hearing Villon's plans to create haute-couture women's shoes, decided to go into partnership with him. That's when the trouble began.

These are the facts. A dispute arose between Ferrebourg and Villon as to where the store should be located. Villon was adamant that the shop be located in the University quarter on the Left Bank with the road of Orleans bringing in foot traffic from the Porte St. Jacques, which became the Grant Rue St. Jacques, the area of most of Villon's Paris life, driving across the Petit-Pont and the Pont Notre-Dame. Ferrebourg was equally as adamant about wanting the store to be located beneath the walls of the Louvre since, he said, he believed that eventually that site would be a "pyramid of business." Of course, no one knew what he was talking about at the time. As is often the case between and among business partners, the disagreement turned violent. Ferrebourg shoved Villon to the pavement and the latter, in a rage, pulled a knife. As Ferrebourg reached for the knife he slipped on the cobblestone street and impaled himself on Villon's blade. Villon's criminal past was to haunt him as he was accused of willfully stabbing Ferrebourg, resulting in his being arrested and sentenced to be "hanged and strangled."

Based on an appeal by Villon's advocate and occasional troubadour, R. Zimmerman, Parliament came up with the following decision on 5 January 1462: "The Court having considered the case brought by the Provost of Paris and his Lieutenant against Master François Villon, and the latter having appealed from the sentence of hanging and strangling: It is finally ordered that the said appeal, and the sentence preceding, be annulled, and having regard to the bad character of the said Villon, that he be banished for ten years from the Town, Rovosty, and Discounty of Paris."

What no one knew was where Villon disappeared to for all those years and the answer lies in the *Jangleresse*: Brazil. Apparently, Villon set sail from Cherbourg to Brazil to learn the techniques of shoe leather-making and opened his own women's shoe store in Sao Paulo in 1467.

He ran the shop until his death in 1501. At that time, his son, François, continued the business until he died in 1575 and his son, Robert, decided to move back to Paris and continue the business, where it flourishes today at the corner of rue Bonaparte and rue de Four.

PART III
Of Stores Miscellaneous

Balzac's Balls

Newport Beach

Balzac, of course, did everything he could think of to make money. Even though he died practically bankrupt, he never gave up the illusion that some day he'd be as rich as Sir Walter Scott, even though Scott too had squandered most of all he had made. Balzac was involved in a number of get-rich schemes, from placing ads in his novels and publishing bogus originals of Molière to buying all the tickets to his play *Les Ressources de Quinola* only to scalp them at exorbitant prices. And who could forget the scam of having other people write stories to which he'd sign his name? But probably the most off-the-wall scheme invented by Balzac involved balls. Rubber balls. We know from Gautier's journal *La vie donc la fou* (1883) that in the little-known book titled *C'est Une Autre Paire de Manches* (1867),[44] published when James Naismith was but a five-year-old Canadian, Michel Peteur writes that it was actually Théophile Gautier not James Naismith who invented the game of basketball, that Balzac was present at its inception. In an attempt to exploit the idea and cash in on what he envisioned as a product that would eventually have an enormous world market (Balzac was prescient here) he came up with the idea of capitalizing on what would become a world famous sport...basketball. As Peteur records, Gautier was in the process of writing his famous poem "Chercher de la Fesse" when his good friend and colleague, Gérald Nerval, burst into Gautier's *atelier*. Immediately, Nerval began hounding Gautier, in typically Nervalian fashion, about what the poet was writing, to which Gautier responded, "rien." Nerval, whose fragile psyche could never accept "rien" as an answer, kept harassing Gautier until the latter, frustrated, finally stood up and crumpled the manuscript as Nerval tried desperately to secure the poem from Gautier's grasp. After a lot of bumping, hand-checking, and fast-breaking up and down the *atelier*, the taller Gautier stopped, jumped into the air and flung the crumpled page over Nerval's outstretched arms. The paper arched over the stiffened defense of the shorter poet, bounced off a nearby wall, spun around the rim of a broken urn, which rested precariously on top of a cluttered oak bookshelf, and plopped in.

Suddenly, it occurred to Gautier at the instant the poem dropped into the urn just what kind of game he had created: a game that necessitated finesse, deft hand-eye coordination, and a bit of Gallic bravura. Peteur writes that at that moment Gautier turned to Nerval and exclaimed, "C'est un jeu d'adresse, de hasard!" Nerval, Peteur writes, merely shrugged his shoulders and left the *atelier* to walk his lobster, Manon, on a pink leash. Gautier knew a popular game when he saw one and so, with Nerval as his assistant, he set out to select a team that would travel the French countryside playing this new game which he originally called "boule de texte," subsequently renamed "basket-malaise" by Baudelaire and, lastly, "basketball" by Naismith.

In order to recruit players, Gautier held tryouts on a sandlot in the Bois de Boulogne. He advertised the tryouts in all sorts of periodicals, both literary and non-literary. Periodicals such as *La Pedale, Le Vieux Schnoque, Broteur*. Needless to say, the turnout was enormous. Poets from throughout the cities and provinces showed up, each attempting to make the team. Members of the prose community were eager to see what kind of "new fangled" idea Gautier was about to launch, an idea to which the oversexed, but non-athletic, Balzac toothlessly replied, "Tu parles d'une idee á la con."

Indeed, it was Balzac who, on 31 March 1840, witnessing some of the early scrimmages Gautier held at the Jeu de Paume, coined the phrase "March madness." The phrase, of course, was a *double entendre* clearly alluding to Nerval's apparent insanity as well as the craziness of the sport, but the term has stuck to this day, being a registered trademark of the NCAA. What Balzac envisioned was a company that produced balls. Rubber balls. The idea so obsessed Balzac that a number of his novels were either titled with the word "ball" in it or alluded to "balls" in the novels themselves. Take, for example, *Le Bal de sceaux* or *La Maison chat qui pelote* or *Le peau de chagrin* (which was originally titled *Le peau de bal*) or *Les Deux Rêves* (which was originally titled, *Les Deux Bals*). Balzac was convinced of the tremendous possibilities of rubber balls and in a letter dated 3 February 1849, to Gautier, the actual inventor of basketball, he proposed a joint venture called Balzac's Balls. Gautier, a good friend of Balzac's but cautious about Balzac's ideas, reluctantly agreed, though contracts were drawn with major escape clauses should Gautier have need for them.

As Balzac's luck would have it, he died in 1850 before the first Balzac's Balls stand was to be inaugurated on the rue de Arbalete between the Panthéon and the Val du Grâce. Before he died, Gautier consigned his percentage to Mallarmé who, while on a lecture tour of the United States, cut a deal with Naismith, who opened the first Balzac's Balls franchise in the Rocky Ripple area of Indianapolis. It remained there until the late 1980s when the franchise moved to the west coast where the acceptance of multicolored balls was more in fashion.[45] The franchise is now located at Fashion Island, Newport Beach, California, where the surfeit of multi-colored balls is only secondary to the plethora of suntanned breasts. It should be noted, however, that before Balzac died, he wrote in his will that a percentage of the profits from the Balzac's Balls franchises be channeled into the creation of coffee shops. Before Mallarmé died, he agreed to a partnership with a distant relative of Heinrich Heine, Rainer Heine, whose success with brewing Heineken Beer led the latter to create the Balzac Coffee shops that are still located in Hamburg.

Beckett's Government Surplus

Norwich

Beckett had joined the Resistance in 1941. That is to say, in 1941 Beckett became a part of the Resistance, a part of the Resistance which he had joined in 1941, 1941 being the year he involved himself in the Resistance, the cell of which was labeled Gloria SMH. HMS backwards. Gloria SMH, not to be confused with HMS Gloria, letters of a different order indeed, indeed a different order.

Beckett worked as a secretary, a liaison, a secretary. A description: Of Beckett. Beckett was well built. Built well. Of virtue. Considerable. But stooped. Had he not been stooped he would have appeared straight. Had he appeared straight he would have appeared more well-built than he was. But not standing straight, that is, stooping, his well-builtness was not easily discerned. Dark hair. Hair dark. But did the darkness precede the hair or did the hair precede the darkness? And did the hair, dark hair, dark as it was to those who noticed it, recede? In other words, if the hair preceded the darkness, was there any evidence of recession? None was spoken of so all that could be surmised was that the hair, dark as it was, was dark first. His fresh complexion was complex indeed, but held no notice beyond the realm of freshness. Beckett was very silent. A Paris agent he. More precisely, Beckett's work entailed typing and translating information reports, reports of information about troop progress, military maneuvers, and others, others and et cetera. While typing these reports, Beckett wore a greatcoat, still green here and there, while typing these reports on a typewriter that had black ribbon. The ribbon worked itself in clockwise fashion as Beckett typed the reports. It was a clean ribbon, not to be confused with unclean ribbon, the latter of which did not type well. Well enough for the ribbon to type cleanly. In clockwise fashion the ribbon worked, blackening the paper on which Beckett typed the reports. Beckett typed, on the table, on a manual typewriter, of greenish color. This excellent typewriter had belonged to his grandfather,[46] who had picked it up, at a government surplus store, from where it was used, by other typists, and took it home. Then gray, now it was greenish, in color.

But Beckett had always remembered that store, the store from which his grandfather had bought the typewriter, for it became the typewriter that he typed the reports of information about troop progress, military maneuvers, and others, et cetera and others that became the basis of his manuscripts. Enamored of the typewriter and of the store from which his grandfather bought it, he bought it. The store. So that others could, perhaps, find typewriters to type on which, in some sundry way, might assist them in the typing of their own reports of information or manuscripts.

Borges' Travel

Tustin

One only needs to read such magnificent short stories as "Tlön Uqbar, Orbis Tertius" or "Death and the Compass" or even "Utopia of a Tired Man" to realize that Borges would eventually expand those artistic interests in travel into something less metaphysical and more lucrative. That's clear from a 1973 chat Borges had with fellow Argentine writer Julio Cortázar at the Café Tortoni in Buenos Aires. At that time, Borges reminded Cortázar, "Let us admit it. Selling short stories is not going to help our retirement. As for me, I have always been fascinated by travel, especially to exotic lands, and I can think of no better kind of vocation than to become a travel agent" (*The Tortoni Chats* 1973). Knowing of Cortázar's interest in music, especially jazz, Borges recommended that the younger writer look for a rock band which would make him some "retirement money." Cortázar heeded Borges' advice and after writing the short story "The Axolotyl," founded a pop group with a similar name. But it was soon after the Tortoni interview that Borges founded his travel agency in his old Buenos Aires neighborhood among "los calles" Guatemala & Serrano, Paraguay & Gurruchaga.

Originally he called the agency "Averroe's Search," but soon after changed it to Borges' Travel when too many people confused the name with a lost-and-found service. The business flourished and actually helped pay for a number of publications of Borges' short stories, including "The Garden of the Forking Paths" and "The Circular Ruins," both of which have travel components to their textual apparatus. Not long after the agency opened, the "travel bug" hit Borges badly and was responsible for his many labyrinthine journeys which took him into and out of "El Aleph" and, according to Dr. Brodie's Report, was responsible for many of his extraordinary tales. But it was on his first visit to Disneyland™ in 1966 (which, by the way, was the origin for the creatures in his *Book of Imaginary Beings*) that Borges decided to franchise the agency when he fell in love with the sleepy little village of Tustin, California. Though there were, at first, a number of problems to be ironed out by the store manager, Don Isidro Parodi, once those six problems were solved, the agency boomed.

According to the chronicles of Bustos Domecq,[47] in keeping with Borges' passion for visiting foreign places, the agency eventually booked a plot for *el maestro* in La Recoleta Cemetery in Buenos Aires, but Borges, always a plot innovator, opted instead to be buried at the Cimetiere des Rois, in Geneva, Switzerland, because those who were to live among him were, he said, better travelers.

To this day, the original store remains in the sleepy village of Tustin, California, and in keeping with a kind of poetic solidarity, books all trips for all artists not only included in this collection, but in the sequel, *Balzac's Coffee, da Vinci's Motel.*

CERVANTES INSTITUTE

Orange

After the initial publishing of *Don Quixote*, Cervantes fell into a kind of postpartum depression. After all, it was Cervantes' life's work which suddenly was lost to him. One could not blame his despondency solely on the publication of *Don Quixote* since the novel met with popular success. On the other hand, perhaps it was the book's lack of financial success that was cause for alarm, for even though it was critically well-received, *Don Quixote* was not going to make Cervantes enough money to dock a yacht in Mallorca. Those who knew him best believed the depression was due to an accumulation of so many tragedies in his life: his physical disability, his enslavement, his imprisonment, his bungled finances, and the major tragedy of having his plays rejected.[48]

By 1611, it was clear no one wanted to stage Cervantes' plays and his financial situation had deteriorated to the point his family was forced to move into the rather squalid conditions on the Calle de León in Madrid. Faced with the realization that his plays would probably never be staged, that *Don Quixote Pt II* was still in-progress, and little was to be gained financially from his other prose, Cervantes considered the idea of becoming a therapist. This idea came at the suggestion of the Count of Lemos, Viceroy of Naples, who occasionally patronized (in the good sense) Cervantes. It was the Count who suggested there was no one more capable of dealing with the psychological problems inherent in the vicissitudes of male menopause found in *Don Quixote* than Cervantes himself. Though Cervantes was reluctant to embark on such a venture, the Count offered to donate funds toward the creation of a Cervantes Institute devoted to dealing with psychological problems associated with male mid-life crisis.

In 1614, the doors to the Cervantes Institute were opened and the venture became an immediate success. Cervantes quit writing fiction and devoted his creative energies to writing self-help books on a variety of subjects such as *The Jealous Extremaduran* (which dealt with new-age methods of dealing with jealousy), *The Illustrious Kitchen Maid* (devoted to improving self-esteem for domestic economists), and *The Deceitful Marriage* (a book devoted to how to recognize and correct potential marital problems). The books all became paperback best-sellers and even outsold *Don Quixote*. However, the therapy and the writing took a physical toll on the aging Cervantes, and before he died he relinquished the rights to his dearest friend, Cide Hamete Benengeli, who began to franchise the institute throughout Spain, then South America and Mexico and, finally, to California, where today, almost four centuries after its inception, it continues to promote mental health in Orange, California, across the street from Papa Hassan's restaurant, the owner of which, coincidentally, is a distant relative of...Cide Hamete Benengeli.

Hemingway's Garage

Santa Ana

Who wouldn't have expected Hemingway to open a garage? What else would a man of such physical strength, of such undiluted machismo, do? At one time Hemingway thought of opening a clothing establishment which catered to matadors. That idea, of course, he considered after publishing *Death in the Afternoon*, but the thought of possibly witnessing some of his best customers being gored to death wearing garments he sold them altered even his steely sensibilities. Actually, it was Dos Passos who suggested that Hemingway open a garage since the idea coincided with what Dos Passos called, "Hemingway's dirty nails" (*Correspondence* 26), a comment made shortly before the Dos Passos-Hemingway rift over the Spanish Civil War. Wrote Dos Passos: "In what other line of work can you be an arbiter for the common man? A good mechanic is like a God, able to resurrect from the disabled that which becomes abled" (*Correspondence* 26). The idea of being like "a God" fascinated the extraordinarily ego-centric Hemingway and the Newtonian notion of controlling the universe in one's hands prompted him to hire "classical mechanics" Nick Adams, Jake Barnes, Frederic Henry, Richard Cantwell, and Thomas Hudson (all of whom had similar mechanical interests) to begin the garage. Hemingway's ultimate goal was to "take the crew to the Indy 500" and "have that crazy fucking Serb (i.e., Vukovich) drive it home." This desire of his can be seen in such early short stories as, "Gasoline Alley" (1936) and "A Clean, Well-Lit Pit Stop" (1937) and as late as "Peanuts on the Chassis" (1957), "Borg-Warner" (1958), and "The Short Happy Life of Bill Vukovich" (1959) written before Hemingway's suicide and after Vukovich's tragic accident. The mechanics who knew him best have said that Hemingway's failure to get to the Indianapolis 500 and "win the fucking thing" was one of the chief reasons for his suicide. Notes recently discovered at the Mayo Clinic after Hemingway's release, and lately published[49] in Mayo's *Journal of Postmortem Fiction* would attest to that desire. One note in particular read: "The Nobel Prize ain't shit compared to Indy. One 500 victory is worth a dozen of them fucking prizes!" Not only does the garage still flourish in Santa Ana, California, but with the success of the garage, Hemingway opened a café in Laguna Beach and became partners with Bertolt Brecht, whose Brecht BMW franchise is one of the most lucrative in Escondido (see *Balzac's Coffee, da Vinci's Motel*).

Notre-Dame & The Hunchback

Paris

Hugo was never very poor. Nor was he short of recognition. So this article is more of an *homage* to what actually happened to Notre-Dame and the hunchback who used to live there. At the age of fifteen, Hugo had already been acknowledged by the French Academy for his poetry, and by seventeen he had won awards from the Jeux floraux de Toulouse. And, perhaps, because of that success the problem for Hugo was not so much to make money, but how to invest it. And that need to diversify established one of the most fascinating events in literary history. As most everyone is well aware, the mature Hugo was extremely interested in the metaphysical and at the age of fifty he became intrigued by séances. Coincidentally, it was at the same time he went into exile from France due, in large measure, to his vilification of Louis Napoléon. In 1853, exiled with his family (i.e., wife, children, mistress), Hugo retreated to the British Isles, first to Jersey then to Guernsey. It was in Guernsey that the table-rapping séances began.

At first, the séances proved fruitless. That is, nothing happened except for a lot of table rapping, which merely resulted in headaches for the *maestro*. As a matter of fact, he was reputed to have said after the first séance, "Ça ne vaut pas un pet de lapin" or "how disappointing." But after continued séances a spirit did speak to him. In fact, it was his dead daughter, Léopoldine, and her message was truly prophetic. These séances were all documented and one of the most mysterious of messages Hugo received from his daughter was the following, "Quasimodo will leave Notre-Dame for Anaheim."[50] The statement initially made no sense to Hugo, who had visited Anaheim (located in the Ruhr Valley of Germany), but only on his way to Warsaw as part of a book tour. He virtually dismissed the statement until 1876 when, after being elected to the Senate, he met, in Paris, at the Café Dauphin, an American by the name of Rudolph Eisner, who said he represented a fledgling cartoon company[51] in the United States. Now film was merely in its fetal stages in France as Lumière and Méliès were not to have produced anything for another decade, but Eisner was interested in making an animated cartoon out of Hugo's *Notre-Dame de Paris* (1831). Hugo was rather fascinated by the idea and asked Eisner where this company was located.

"Burbank," he said, "but that's where our studio is. We plan to build a theme park in California."

"Where?" Hugo asked.

"Anaheim," was the answer.

And Hugo suddenly remembered the prophetic words of his dead daughter, "Quasimodo will leave Notre Dame for Anaheim and will then reside in the hills of Beverly." Flushed with the idea that his novel would be adapted to an animated cartoon, Hugo worked out the contractual arrangements with Eisner and a date was set for production.[52] But Hugo was still mystified by the future residence of Quasimodo in the hills of Beverly. What could that mean?

Almost six years later, 1882, Hugo sent his mistress, Juliette Drouet, to the United States to do some advanced booking for his latest novel *Torquemada*. When Eisner discovered she was in New York, he arranged for her to come to California to see the Willie Studios and to view what progress had been made on what had now been re-titled *Willie's Hunchback of Notre Dame*. She agreed. In a letter dated 2 December 1882, postmarked Burbank, Juliette writes Hugo: "Good morning, my divine, adored love. This separation spares me no sorrow. Being away from you is like being rendered soulless, joyless, loveless, but I do these things for you not out of gratitude, but out of my strongest, deepest love for you. Monsieur Eisner has shown me the animated drawings of Quasimodo. Somehow I do not think them what you had in mind, but he tells me that is what the American public wants. Que dommage. He has also mentioned something to me about a restaurant in Beverly Hills, but I shall find out more later. My darling, this separation cannot be over too soon and I pray your love will take me from here to there with speed and sanctity. I love you, Juliette."

The restaurant Drouet alluded to was actually going out of business and Eisner convinced Hugo, through Drouet, to invest in it with the sound reasoning that it would diversify Hugo's portfolio. So convinced, he did in fact invest and the restaurant opened as the Victor Hugo Restaurant in 1883, the exact day Juliette Drouet died. If that were not irony enough, the restaurant burned to the ground in 1885, on the exact day Hugo was buried in the Panthéon. Some say it was the spirit of Quasimodo that burned the restaurant as an homage to the *maestro* since witnesses swear that on the night of fire they saw a hunchback rushing from the burning building. Others attest it was done by a disgruntled Willie employee who was fired after an altercation with the head of the animation studio who proclaimed that he had pornographized all that Willie had done.[53] In either case, all that remained was a matchbook cover which has since found its way into the Smithsonian.

But the spirit of Quasimodo lived on and not to everyone's liking. Certainly not the Hugo family and a relatively recent letter, signed by Charles, Adèle, Jeanne, Sophie, and Léopoldine Hugo, denounced the "commercial debauchery which confuses the universality of genius with vulgar globalization by unscrupulous merchants." As Adèle Hugo-Chabrol said, "We are not after money. We are in favor of screen adaptations because they help new readers discover the author. But this time, Victor Hugo is not even mentioned on the posters." Alas, it was true. Nowhere on any of the film posters of *The Hunchback of Notre-Dame* was Hugo's name mentioned, which was in direct violation of the codicil that Hugo had signed with Rudolph Eisner.[54] Needless to say, the current Disney™ legal conundrum was in direct violation of that testimony. What of Quasimodo's status? The fact is that the "cuddly" Quasimodo has taken up residence in a *ménage à trois* in Beverly Hills with a D. Moore and her husband not only testifies to that violation, but, in a macabré sort of way, brings Léopoldine's prophecy to fruition. And Notre-Dame de Paris? It has become a tourist attraction where they sell Quasimodo merchandise.

D.H. Lawrence's Detectives, Inc.

Irvine

687 Orange County LAWLER-LAWYERS L

Lawler Willard 285 W Central Av Brea ... 256 2853
LAWLER WILLIAM E MD
1211 W La Palma Av Anh ... 520 5661
Lawler William E MD 3010 W Orange Av Anh ... 826 9320
Lawler Wm H 2821 Anacapa Pl Ful ... 870 6635
Lawless Brian L 320 N Orange LH ... 310 691 7560
Lawless Catherine 8606 Solano Cir HB ... 960 6340
Lawless I 11253 Gardinrs Ct Cyp ... 894 1940
Lawless J HB ... 843 5218
Lawless James W 5228 Cumberland Dr Cyp ... 527 3480
Lawless Michael J & Elizabeth ... 441 1659
Lawless Roger E 2545 Robinhood Pl Org ... 998 5585
Lawless William & Missy ... 644 8806
Lawley Bonnie K atty 2555 E Chapman Av Ful ... 526 6650
Lawley Mark David 457-3rd Lag B ... 494 0739
Lawley Robert 2760 Associated Rd Ful ... 529 7994
Lawlor James & Toni ... 635 6159
Lawlor Michael E DDS 331 N Harbor Bl LH ... 310 694 3511
Lawlor Noel 17612 Jordan Av Irv ... 551 4285
Lawlor Roger E 1526 E Avalon Av SA ... 547 2781
Lawman 2024 N Broadway SA ... 667 0561
Lawmaster S T ... 778 3309
Lawn Butler ... 630 6333
Lawn Club P O Box 4747 GG ... 533 7500
Lawn Heather Lynn astrlgr 1200 Quail NB ... 752 6160
Lawn Sheriff The ... 559 0119
Lawner Stephan 413 S Clara SA ... 541 1129
Lawnmower Shop 13331 Brookhurst GG ... 539 6165
Lawnscape Systems Inc ... 800 255 5296
Lawrence A Carl 7642 Arroyo Cir La Plma ... 310 865 2659
Lawrence A P 138 Coronado Ln Tus ... 547 5985
Lawrence Al L & Andrea 1225 N Van Buren Plac ... 996 2161
Lawrence Alan & Naomi ... 642 1912
Lawrence B ... 733 3706
Lawrence B Bonas Co 1301 Hunter Av SA ... 953 2010
Lawrence B George 21851 Newlnd HB ... 969 9720
Lawrence Beebe Co 485 E-17th CM ... 548 0131
Lawrence Beebe Co 485 E-17th CM ... 650 7427
From Santa Ana Telephones Call ... 850 0100
Lawrence Billy C 8302 San Marino Dr Bu Pk ... 952 4891
Lawrence Brian W ... 644 4736
Lawrence C HB ... 536 7654
Lawrence C ... 871 7269
Lawrence C A 4211 Greenwood Av Org ... 538 1506
Lawrence C H 14302 East Mall Irv ... 552 0680
Lawrence C L ... 708 2289
Lawrence Carl H ... 894 3862
Lawrence Carl & Veronica ... 838 2625
Lawrence Carroll E & Ethel 8448 E Hillsdale Dr Org ... 771 9007
Lawrence Charles ... 491 1740
Lawrence Chas ... 962 5298
Lawrence Charles & Tricia ... 283 0423
Lawrence Chuck 5271 Auburn Cir Wmstr ... 891 4247
Lawrence Chuck E 16669 Redwood F Vly ... 839 3974
Lawrence Clint ... 545 5175
Lawrence Connie Lag B ... 376 9077
Lawrence D Lag B ... 376 9507
Lawrence D ... 521 7528
Lawrence D J ... 996 2320
Lawrence D P 915 E Palmyra Av Org ... 771 4242
Lawrence Dale E ... 828 8653
Lawrence Dana 808 Quivera Lag B ... 499 0930
Lawrence Dave ... 638 4909
Lawrence David ... 638 9786
Lawrence David 14132 Roxanne Dr Wmstr ... 892 2036
Lawrence David A 507 S Wrightwood Org ... 639 9933
Lawrence David E ... 539 2187
Lawrence David J & Roberta 3530WSweetbayCt Anh ... 826 0117
Lawrence Denise ... 827 8721
Lawrence Dennis & Ruth HB ... 842 9601
Lawrence Design Atelier 25131 Calle Playa Lag Nigl ... 831 6632
Lawrence Detectives Inc HB ... 846 4488
Lawrence Detectives Inc ... 310 276 6303
Lawrence Detectives Inc 19200VonKarmanAv Irv 818 343 7563

Lawrynowicz Danl 180 Coronel Lag B ... 376 1873
Laws A C GG ... 895 2602
Laws Bonnie D DVM 1826 N Tustin Org ... 637 3660
Laws C R ... 777 5116
Laws Co Ltd The 1300 Bristol Street North NB ... 252 0606
Laws Dean R ... 673 6183
Laws Donald 7815-15th Wmstr ... 897 5233
Laws Doris M 612 S Paula Av Ful ... 526 4775
Laws H Vickrey 3050 W Ball Rd Anh ... 826 7515
Laws Jette & Don 34 N Portola Lag B ... 499 0292
Law's John Bowling Supply 201 S Brookhurst Anh ... 776 0391
Laws K ... 839 2615
Laws Raymon L Jr Bu Pk ... 522 5504
Laws Roy J 182 Rochester CM ... 548 5846
Laws Wilbur T 2454 Shadow Ridge Ln Org ... 998 1803
Laws Willa ... 548 4648
Lawson A ... 521 3844
Lawson A ... 539 0169
Lawson A & D Whit ... 310 691 6248
Lawson Alan D ... 441 2853
Lawson Associates 121 W Hidden Ln LH ... 310 905 3446
Lawson Associates Inc 3333 Michelson Dr Irv ... 975 0150
Lawson B ... 723 4715
Lawson Bill ... 545 3796
Lawson Bill ... 751 8248
Lawson Bonnie ... 870 1040
Lawson Bonnie 17257 Snta Lucie F Vly ... 847 3457
Lawson Brett & Carleen ... 521 5656
Lawson C ... 731 1502
Lawson Carl P 811 W Royal Wy Anh ... 535 6869
Lawson Carol ... 680 8641
Lawson Catherine J Md ... 631 0616
Ofc 20311 Acacia NB
Lawson Catherine J MD 20311 Acacia NB ... 852 1500
Lawson Chas M 2701 Starbird Dr CM ... 751 4473
Lawson Chester David & Kathleen ... 522 0226
Lawson Clayton W ... 832 8082
Lawson Curt ... 542 7977
Lawson D ... 559 5282
Lawson D ... 673 3110
Lawson D ... 832 6660
Lawson D F Vly ... 964 0512
Lawson D L 270 Cagney Ln NB ... 650 4550
Lawson Darrell L 5196 Mountain View Av YL ... 777 2255
Lawson Daryl Rev & Debra ... 662 1744
Lawson Dave 6272 Royl Oak Dr HB ... 897 5694
Lawson Dave & Yolanda 4426 Avenida Del Este YL ... 777 4450
Lawson David & Julia ... 642 5589
Lawson David M 125 N College LH ... 310 691 4007
Lawson Denise 2578 Associated Rd Ful ... 525 4824
Lawson Devin 420-21st HB ... 960 7877
Lawson Diane M ... 642 4888
Lawson Don & Carol 3241 La Travesia Dr Ful ... 526 4881
Lawson Donald E MD 10382 Miralago Pl SA ... 544 4497
Lawson E ... 673 3668
Lawson E 3919 W Garden Grove Bl Org ... 971 2231
Lawson E G 343 W Amerige Av Ful ... 992 6818
Lawson E J HB ... 969 8491
Lawson Edw 8200 Bolsa Av M Cty ... 895 3336
Lawson Electric 675 N Eckhoff Org ... 939 7680
Lawson Elvin E 6832 Oregon Bu Pk ... 521 6456
Lawson Emmet 18751 Fairhaven Av SA ... 538 2401
Lawson Eric ... 550 7502
Lawson Estate The 2713 W Coast Hwy NB ... 646 3599
Lawson F Jas 17122 Bluewatr Ln HB ... 310 592 2557
Lawson Frank ins 285 E Main Tus ... 731 6381
Lawson Frank M 1595 N Milford Org ... 532 1180
Lawson Gary HB ... 960 7819
Lawson Gary 18180 Devnwd Cir F Vly ... 968 6473
Lawson Gary & C 9252 Imperial Av GG ... 537 4317
Lawson Gary & Debra 1013 Mammoth Wy Plac ... 524 6546
Lawson George M & Peggy ... 970 8950
Lawson Gerald 13100 E Firestne Bl S F Sps ... 310 802 0776
Lawson Group The 3745 W Chapman Av Org ... 978 7107

Lawson Nat & Phyllis 5191 Corni Av Wmstr ... 898 0589
Lawson Norman B Co ... 646 4471
Res ... 642 4888
Lawson Paul ... 540 6683
Lawson Paul 1531 W Chanticleer Rd Anh ... 635 5173
Lawson Paul E 759 S Goldfinch Wy Anh ... 281 1380
Lawson Paul & Sharon ... 538 5847
Lawson R ... 505 0665
Lawson R D 10 Crystl Cove Lag B ... 494 2480
Lawson R W ... 857 0093
Lawson Refrigeration Heating & AC
14252 Culver Dr Irv ... 552 3130
Lawson Richard E & Dorothea ... 535 0642
Lawson Rick D 1859 N Diamond Org ... 921 1254
Lawson Robt 18832 Florida HB ... 842 0525
Lawson Robt 1051 Site Dr Brea ... 529 1710
Lawson Robt E 2105 S Hammatt Pkwy Anh ... 638 0645
Lawson Robt & Jean Lag B ... 494 3054
Lawson Robert Structural Engineers
312 Ocean Av Lag B ... 494 0776
Lawson Roger D 16562 Fountn Ln HB ... 842 3655
Lawson Ron D 20282 Avenida Puesta Del Sol YL ... 970 5493
Lawson Ron Jr ... 545 4634
Lawson Ronald ... 537 6446
Lawson S HB ... 965 2321
Lawson S HB ... 965 2610
Lawson S K 1414 Century Dr Org ... 633 5207
Lawson S K 5151 Walnut Av Irv ... 552 9082
Lawson Sally HB ... 969 7272
Lawson Sally & Bob 8471 Gilfrd Cir HB ... 962 3042
Lawson Scott ... 529 0742
Lawson Scott LB ... 962 9120
Lawson Screen Products Inc
1541 N Orangethorpe Wy Anh ... 525 9300
Lawson Sheila Lag B ... 499 4616
Lawson Shelby ... 774 5114
Lawson & Smith Attorneys At Law 1851 E-1st SA ... 541 4454
Lawson Steve ... 995 5747
Lawson Steve 707 E Erna Av LH ... 310 697 0512
Lawson Steve & Patricia Wmstr ... 891 4001
Lawson T A ... 528 6549
Lawson T A ... 957 1689
Lawson Thos Wmstr ... 843 6170
Lawson Thos E 1729 Saint James Pl Plac ... 993 6883
Lawson Thos W 801 N Glassell Org ... 538 1453
Lawson Thos Wmstr ... 848 2850
Lawson Todd ... 563 1577
Lawson Tom ... 870 7560
LAWSON TOM INSURANCE AGENCY INC
115 S Harbor Bl Ful ... 870 4342
Lawson V ... 524 2479
Lawson V M ... 731 5883
Lawson Vicki ... 952 8961
Lawson W D 1859 N Glassell Org ... 637 2724
Lawson W G 121 W Hidden Ln LH ... 310 697 7049
Lawson Walter A HB ... 840 8906
Lawson William A III atty 1851 E-1st SA ... 541 4454
Lawson Wm E 931 W Wilson CM ... 548 1536
Lawson Wm F 6570 Grand Manan Dr Cyp ... 897 7192
Lawson Wm H III & Martha 44 Choate Irv ... 551 9782
Lawson's Gardens 8620 Hamilton HB ... 969 3875
Lawson's Landscape 8620 Hamiltn Av HB ... 969 8995
Lawsons Landscape Services 6 Morgan Irv ... 707 1236
Lawther Bob & Betty 240 Waterwheel Ln Brea ... 256 2104
Lawther Fredrick 18132 Ivorycrst Ln HB ... 848 9522
Lawther K A 2663 Dietrich Dr Tus ... 505 3517
Lawton C ... 549 0872
Lawton Carll ... 879 8709
Lawton D ... 283 1153
Lawton D & L 1241 N East St Anh ... 870 7274
Lawton Frank C 14851 Jeffrey Rd Irv ... 552 4734
Lawton Irwin E Dr ... 535 1654
Lawton J ... 857 1789
Lawton Jas E 5318 E Pamela Kay Ln Anh ... 998 5195
Lawton Joseph S MD 100 E Valencia Mesa Dr Ful ... 871 1200

Not long after World War I began in Europe, Lawrence set out to create a new utopia which he called Ranamin. The origins of the word are sketchy, though it seems he created a *portmanteau* from the words of an Old Testament psalm. It was a curious derivation indeed given Lawrence's penchant for anti-Semitism and Jew baiting, which was really the thrust behind starting his detective agency in the first place. You see, while Lawrence was attempting to formulate a charter for his utopia, he wrote the following letter to Lady Caroline Morrell:

"It is communism based, not on poverty, but riches, not on humility, but on pride, not on sacrifice, but upon complete fulfillment in the flesh of all strong desire, not on forfeiture but upon inheritance, not on heaven but on earth. We will be Sons of God who walk here on earth, not bent on getting and having, because we know we inherit all things. We will be aristocrats, as wise as the serpent in dealing with the mob. For the mob shall not crush us nor starve us nor try us to death. We will deal cunningly with the mob, the greedy soul, we will gradually bring it to subjection. We will found an order, and we will be Princes, as the angels are. We must bring this about—at least set it into *life*, bring it forth newborn on the earth, watched over by our old cunning and guided by our ancient, mercenary-soldier habits."

The key word here is "the mob" since Lawrence was, above all else, paranoid of "the other," the other being "women" (re-read *Women in Love)*, and "Jews" (re-read *Virgin and the Gypsy*) or, for that matter, any of the hoi-polloi. In short, what he was fashioning was a neo-fascist colony. So, before he could create Ranamin in his own image, he had to be perfectly sure about those whom he was going to invite to the colony which, as we now know, really was to be a neo-fascist art colony. Hence the creation of the Lawrence Detective Agency (as it was originally called) which he began with extensive loans from prominent London banks.

Lawrence was so obsessed with the idea his writing began to suffer. But the thought of making money (regardless of his "anti-materialist posture") and in finding the "right people" for Ranamin became the sole reasons for his existence. With the assistance of several of his friends (including E.M. Forster), Lawrence opened his agency in Wimbledon in 1918 and quickly ran "Personality Profiles" on scads of people he thought would be unsuitable for Ranamin. He ran so many profiles that eventually the number was so huge it finally led to the creation of an in-house UnRanamic Activities Section (HuRA, for short). Jews, Communists, Communist Jews, Jews with Communist friends, friends of Gentiles, Gentiles with Jewish friends, friends of Gentiles with Communist friends, friends who may have been literary agents, literary agents associated with publishers who didn't think his work was magnificent, and every other permutation of which one might be able to conceive were all profiled.[55]

Soon other businesses and organizations found out about Lawrence's Detective Agency, were interested in what Lawrence was doing and hired the agency to conduct surveillance operations and other clandestine activities. Business boomed. As a matter of fact, business became so good that he was about to give up writing altogether, and based on his last novel *The Virgin and the Gypsy*, it was apparent that Lawrence had lost any interest in writing. Unfortunately for Lawrence, all of this hard work went for naught because in 1930 Lawrence died and after his death there was little the support staff could do without him. Most everyone returned to their own writing and the agency died a slow death in 1931.

But in 1946, shortly after the end of World War II, Joseph McCarthy, on reading the ideas suggested in Lawrence's letters, took up the mantle of "UnRanamic Activities" and, applying the same principles to America, not only blacklisted the same kind of people Lawrence did, but as an homage to Lawrence opened the same kind of detective agency in Lawrence's name. Because McCarthy's brand of public hanging finally became unfashionable, he left Washington and returned to Wisconsin (the agency was originally located in Madison, Wisconsin, at the past site of the Ovens of Brittany Restaurant). Then, for political reasons, he moved the agency first to Hollywood, California (ironically, in the same place Nathanael West lived before McCarthy had him evicted for being both Jewish and a film writer) and then to Reseda.

Eventually, the agency was sold to the well-known D'Annunzio family from Orange County, California, who have kept the business alive to this day. The charge of the agency has changed somewhat, since its focus relies heavily on investigating Orange County residents who are not as bourgeois as the city charter mandates or who may be legal Latinos or have had affiliations with Latinos who may have crossed into the United States illegally or who may know of Latinos who know of Latinos who have entered the United States legally or illegally or who allegedly know Latinos of the same status. However, to a great extent, the overall thrust of the agency has not changed at all and Lawrence would have been happy about that since difference of any persuasion was anathema to him.

Nijinski Bookstore

Brussels

What is clear about why Nijinsky finally opened a bookstore can be traced to his marriage with Romola de Pulszky in Buenos Aires (1913) and the fallout that marriage caused with Diaghilev. Nijinsky had received no salary for three years even though Diaghilev paid for miscellaneous matters. When he was fired by Diaghilev for "refusing to dance" in Rio, Nijinsky had to look for other avenues of income while he tried to reconcile matters with Diaghilev, which never happened.

Returning to Russia was out of the question; an offer in Paris was too constricting; only London received him, but even that was short-lived when he suffered from a nervous breakdown and was hospitalized. While recovering in the hospital, Nijinsky began reading and discovered what a genuine pleasure it was and how much he had missed it. He began reading all the Russians he had read as a child—Tolstoy, Dostoevsky, Pushkin, Turgenev, Gogol, Lermontov, A'kselrad, Goncharov—and started to think about something other than Diaghilev and dance.

What truly convinced him to scrap dance altogether was his trip to the United States. In 1916, a New York performance of *Schéchérazade* was greeted with a news story that read: "Nijinsky Dances. Audience Laughs...Mythological Poem Effeminate Exhibit. Story of Narcissus and the Spring, Told Terpsichorean Fashion, Greeted by Giggles." In addition, Diaghilev continued his vendetta against Nijinsky and tried to blacken his name everywhere and anywhere he could. Nijinsky had enough.

Recalling his days in the hospital, Nijinsky decided that he'd rather submerge himself in a sea of secondhand books than condemn himself to a lifetime of being demonized by Diaghilev. Nijinsky then retired to the languid life of a bookseller, changing the store's name to "Nijinski" (so he would not be annoyed) and remained there until

1950, when he began to suffer from physical ailments. Before his death, he told his daughter Kyra, who subsequently took over the business, that "any book on dance is a welcome addition, but nothing on Diaghilev."[56] The bookstore, which was located in Montmartre, was subsequently bought and moved to Brussels, where it still exists.

REMBRANDT TOOTHPASTE™

Del Mar

If you've ever wondered why no one smiles in Rembrandt's paintings you're not alone. It's because the subjects all had horrible teeth. This void preoccupied Rembrandt for a number of years, but it was only after painting *Night Watch* (1642) that he began contemplating how he could alter that situation since he was deeply depressed over the fact none of his subjects (including himself, as in *Self-Portrait* [1634]) ever smiled and the few Dutch art patrons he had were pressing him to paint something "more lively." At the same time, Rembrandt was suffering from severe financial problems and the threat of bankruptcy loomed on the horizon. The answer to solving both problems came in a most extraordinary way.

With creditors clamoring for money owed them, Rembrandt was on the brink of a financial crisis. He had attempted a number of scams to avoid bankruptcy and to pay off his creditors, but nothing worked. He had his possessions sold, his paintings auctioned and, finally, had his house repossessed even though he tried unsuccessfully to put the deed in his son's name. At the end of his tether, Rembrandt came upon the ingenious idea of creating toothpaste. The same night he finished the master portrait of his son *Titus* (1655) and was preparing him for bed, he asked his son why he didn't enjoy smiling. The young boy said it was because "[his] teeth were yellow." Always imaginative, Rembrandt found some paint and, mixing the appropriate colors the way only he could, dabbed a bit on the child's teeth. Miraculously the paint adhered and the boy's smile returned. Flushed with success, Rembrandt searched for other ingredients to add to the concoction until he finally came up with a formula that made his toothpaste the most popular in the Netherlands and, eventually, all of Western Europe (England was not included here since a flash of yellow teeth was considered a sign of royalty).

Though Rembrandt did not live long enough to reap any of the financial rewards of the product, Titus continued the Research and Development of the product through the 18th century, passing it along to his daughter Titia. The family continued the business until it was eventually sold to a Dutch conglomerate in 1968, which sold off part of its assets to Japanese and American interests in 1987. A vestige of the original company, now called Den-Mat™, operates out of Santa Maria, California, but its mission statement still includes the phrase made famous by Rembrandt so many centuries before, "A day without a white smile is like a day without sunshine."

SHAKESPEARE'S MONOFILAMENTS™
Columbia

Recent scholarship has corroborated what old scholarship had long contended, that Shakespeare (aka Shaksper) had, in fact, nothing literary to do with the plays of the same name and that they were clearly written by Edward DeVere, Seventeenth Earl of Oxford, Lord Great Chamberlain of England, Viscount Bulbeck, Lord Sanford, Lord of Escales and Baldlesmere, Patron of the English Renaissance. Beyond the meaningless and undocumented assertions of homophobic scholars such as A.L. Rowse (whose favorite opprobrium was to call gays "homos"), certain stylistic features and literary allusions point to the fact that indeed it was DeVere who penned those words and Shakespeare's "attributes," that is, being born into an illiterate family, never finishing high school, bearing illiterate children and *not* being buried in Westminster Abbey, do cast a pale over the bard's majestic gifts, lending credence to the line there truly was something rotten in the state of Denmark...or at least in Stratford.

The latest critical text to deal with the issue, specifically Alfonso Baldoni's critically acclaimed *Shakespeare: Gay, Garrulous and Gaitered,* indicates that not only was Shakespeare *not* the author of the plays, but he began a number of questionable forays into business ventures in order to gloss over the fact that, after the last of DeVere's plays were posthumously produced, Shakespeare desperately needed a way to make money. Baldoni writes that Shakespeare actually "cut a deal" with one of DeVere's emissaries to sign his name to the plays because DeVere, a cosmopolitan polyglot, could not have done so himself without major repercussions from the social and regal community of Elizabethan England. DeVere paid Shakespeare handsomely for the use of his name, but Shakespeare knew that after DeVere's death, which occurred in 1604, he'd be up the Thames without a paddle.

According to Baldoni, the notorious blank period in Shakespeare's life while he was in London was not so blank after all. During that time, the illiterate tanner's son was investigating a number of different financial opportunities to replace the money he wouldn't be getting after DeVere's death. During that period, Shakespeare met the Third Earl of Southampton, an alleged homosexual of significant means who, Baldoni suggests, was Shakespeare's lover during those same "blank" years in London. As a matter of fact, Baldoni suggests that what Shakespeare was actually doing during those years when he abandoned his family was parking horses at the theatres. In other words, he was an equine valet.

One of Southampton's keenest interests was, curiously, fishing, and the two of them engaged in fishing trysts from Loch Ness to Windermere whenever Southampton needed time to get away from the rigours of royalty. In those days, the lake country was inundated with plants of all types and sizes, which made it difficult for the pair of anglers to get to the water of their choice. And how to cut down the foliage to get to the water became a crucial concern. "If only there were a way to eliminate the weeds without pulling them out by hand," was what Southampton said in a letter to Shakespeare dated 21 June 1603. That was the question the two of them pondered while at the same time Shakespeare was supposedly writing all those plays; however, it was Southampton's idea that eventually yielded the discovery of the monofilament. That plastic thread which we all know and admire today as being the integral part of the "weed eater" was, in fact, a collaborative invention of both Shakespeare and Southampton.

According to Baldoni, Southampton had begun sketching ways to "cut down the weedes." Using a scythe, of course, was too burdensome, but the idea of incorporating the mechanics of the scythe with something less ponderous, but equally as effective, intrigued him. The idea of using a fibrous filament finally came to him one evening as he was eating celery. He told Shakespeare of the idea and the two of them (as Boldoni indicates it was more Southampton's genius than Shakespeare's) began experimenting with different "celery-like" filaments until they came up with what they originally called the "mono-fylamente." The original "weede eatter" was much smaller than the one used today and was much slower (due, in part, to the smaller voltage of the batteries used at the time).

At Southampton's suggestion, and with his financial support, Shakespeare began his own microfilament company in 1613, creatively called Shakespeare's Lines. As a matter of fact, the bust of the "bard" in Stratford was actually commissioned by Southampton and was, at the time, according to Baldoni, supposed to have Shakespeare holding the handle of the weed eater the two of them had jointly invented. Somehow the person who fashioned the sculpture, a Malcolm Caliban, misread the order, and since the order was for one William Shakespeare of Shakespeare's Lines he assumed "lines" meant written lines, hence the ridiculous posture of Shakespeare holding a quill pen in his hand.

After Shakespeare's death, the company was taken over by his son-in-law and though it has changed hands numerous times over the centuries, the name was changed from "lines" to "monofilaments" so as not to confuse the product with anything like *belles lettres*, but, rather, to be associated with world-class weed eaters. The company is presently located in Columbia, South Carolina.

Axelrod's Toys

La Jolla

D oubtless it was out of both professional and economic frus-
tration that after his 50th birthday (more or less the same
birthday that suffused Von Aschenbach with the need to escape to
Venice and Don Quixote to depart La Mancha) and with little to show
for 30 years of literary effort, Axelrod decided to give up the literary
life altogether and enter the toy business. Toys, of course, were a natural extension of the kind of work Axelrod had been engaged in for
over three decades since most of his work was considered, by those
who knew it best as "light, playful, and jocular," so the transition from
writing fiction to peddling toys was perfect. Works like the feature
novel *Bombay California*; the Castles Trilogy (*Cardboard Castles, Cloud
Castles, Capital Castles*); the innovative *Neville Chamberlain's Chimera and
Dante's Foil and Other Tales*; the uniquely postmodern *The Posthumous
Memoirs of Blase Kubash* and the memorable *Borges' Travel, Hemingway's
Garage* (not to mention all the fiction that was yet unwritten, including
Balzac's Coffee, da Vinci's Motel) all reflected the extraordinary playfulness
of his work. Though the majority of the minority of literary critics
who have even read Axelrod's work have all overlooked the political
nature of it, that oversight was due to the fact everyone ignored him
anyway. However, if they did not ignore him, they would have con-
curred with Axelrod's former college English professor Melvin
Plotinsky, who once called his work "witty" and his former compara-
tive literature professor Claus Clüver, who once asked him, "Did you
really write this stuff?"

In the now famous *Esquire*™ interview with Hunter Thompson,
conducted at a tide pool in La Jolla, California, when asked about his
decision to abandon writing fiction for selling toys, Axelrod, who, at
the time, was walking a battery operated lobster on a pink leash,
responded in a Nervalian way, "Toys don't bark and they know the

secrets of the sea. Besides," he continued, "unlike editors, agents, publishers, and most readers, toys are dependable and can be trusted to be there when you need them. More important, they do it without taking a commission. They may not have life as we understand it, but toys have heart."

Those familiar with his work know that it was not only ignored, but spurned, and that his fiction and graphic work were among the most imaginative in the late twentieth century. Asked by Thompson if he held any grudges, Axelrod replied, quoting Beckett when he was asked in the early '80s why he wasn't considered by *Passion* magazine as one of the top 100 authors living in Paris, "I forgive them."

Though Thompson claims he actually witnessed Axelrod walk into the ocean with the toy lobster, disappearing in the festered foam, witnesses claim to have seen him walking the same lobster on the streets of Santiago de Chile (actually in Providencia, specifically outside the Café Tavelli). Others have claimed they've seen him with Raymond Federman at La Coupole plagiarizing material for future unwritten texts, while still others claim he is actually living in Buenos Aires, having seen him imbibing Malebec at the Café Mahler and consorting with Argentine novelist Luisa Valenzuela, under the alias Macedonio Fernandez, at the Café Tortoni. Regardless of where he is, or what he is now doing, the store itself remains in La Jolla, California, ironically on Girard Avenue, the street where he was born in Philadelphia, which is nestled between the pathos of the Pacific and the pines and the peripatetic breezes that render fiction writers innocuous.

Notes

1. Curiously, in Denmark, Danish pastry is actually called Austrian pastry. So, when one wants Danish in Denmark one should ask for Austrian since asking for Danish will only result in quizzical looks whether spoken in English or Danish. I was informed of this cultural conundrum by the Danish filmmaker, Henning Carlsen.

2. These were actually the notes for *Repetition*.

3. *The Diary of Søren Kierkegaard*, March, 1838.

4. According to records, the name of the pub was originally Milton's, but, apparently Milton wanted out of the pub business and opened a restaurant in Laguna Beach, California, not far from the new Hemingway's Café.

5. In Boswell's "Notes for a Life of Sir Joshua Reynolds" records Reynolds saying that the reason for this interest was because the mixing of drinks in a glass was the closest thing to the mixing of paints on a palette and demanded "as much tangful artistry as colourful brilliance of Botticelli."

6. The barman in Reynolds' youthful hangout, Cheers.

7. *From* The Tartar Steppes *to* The Plague*: The Letters of Dino Buzzati and Albert Camus*. Milan: Einaudi, 1963.

8. Contrary to what has been written about the Sartre-Camus split, the real reason was their differences concerning who would win the 1950 World Cup. Camus, a Brazilian enthusiast, was adamant about their chances of winning; Sartre, on the other hand, was keen on Yugoslavia. Camus was right, Sartre was wrong, hence the schism that Sartre could never quite reconcile.

9. This account was given by one Marcel Camus, a truck driver, present at the time of the accident who said the bottle spun around several times before sliding off the slippery road and falling into a ditch, cap side down. The bottle, he said, was empty. This story was never confirmed.

10. *Minnesota Lips: Lesbians from St. Cloud to Duluth*. White Pearl, MN: Minnesota State Press, 1996.

11. *The Gouine Letters: From Gigi to Colette*. St. Paul, MN: Pearl & Cream Press, 1998.

12. The exact recipe for this dessert is a secret, so one needn't look for it. Apparently, it was created by Colette and the ingredients are passed on in a secret erotic ceremony from one dessert chef to another "under the cloak of sheets and darkness."

13. In his notebooks on the *Inferno*, on a page dated 31 March 1302, Dante writes that he thought of a place far, far away from the strife of Italy and "Santiago comes to mind." He was alluding to Santiago de Chile where, between 1302-1314, he completed the *Inferno* before returning to Romagna.

14. *The Journals of Amerigo Ormea*, Vol. II 1302-1321, published by Einaudi, Milan, 1984. Ormea is probably most well-known for his story "La Giornata d'uno scrutatore," though he had also written "La Nnuvola di smog" and "La Formica chilena."

15. One excerpt from the journal accounts how Dante would wake up at four in the morning and walk to the café, where he would write until the café opened at 6:30. On one such occasion, he witnessed a number of soldiers beating defenseless men, women, and children. When he asked what crime they had committed he was told they were "social outcasts." When he asked what that meant, he was told it meant they stood for "social disorder." When Dante asked by whose authority these people were persecuted, he was told it was the decision of "the most august." The situation so moved him that it became the basis for Canto XXVIII of the *Inferno*.

16. From *Idée Nouvelle: The Life and Works of Frederich Engels*.

17. The film starring Zeppo Marx as Engels and Marty Engels as Marx, and re-titled *Boogie Knights*, was never released.

18. This particular passage is from a telegram Engels sent to Marx, who was, at that time, allegedly recuperating from an illness in Palm Springs, California, but documentation shows he was actually at the Warner Studios in Burbank, signing the necessary contracts.

19. From the *Marx-Engels Correspondence*, published by Thyme-Werner Publications.

20. As the story goes, Mastroianni invited the commissioner, Sandro Abbaiare, to the restaurant to survey the completely naked waitresses, all of whom were waiting for him. Mastroianni greeted Abbaiare at the door and the commissioner was speechless when the former paraded about a dozen beautiful women before him. After every model walked by, Mastroianni would say, "Lei ha delle belle chiappe, no!" Abbaiare, who was a bit "hot under his collar" from the whole thing thought Marcello a bit over the top and with a curt bow exited excitedly, saying as he left, "Non rompermi le palle!" Needless to say, the staff had to alter their costumes.

21. That is to say, the café used to be located on Melrose near the Cinegrill, but has since gone out of business. Speculation was abundant about its demise, but the record is clear from the Los Angeles Department of Sanitation that the café was closed because it was in direct violation of Statute 735.014, "harboring insects as pets." Apparently, at least in California, cockroaches are only allowed to run for political office and may not be used for any other commercial purpose. The only exception to this statute is written in sub-statute number 735.014 (a), which reads that "...if no literary agent exists, cockroaches may be allowed to become literary agents provided the insect has a proper knowledge of literary texts, competence of which will be satisfied by a credentialed exam regulated by the California Governor's office." Totally frustrated with the California code system, the café owners, in an attempt to get as far away from those codes as possible, moved the café to Helsinki, Finland, where, because of the extreme cold, cockroaches cannot flourish.

22. At the time in Germany, cookies were not eaten as they are today, but sucked. Hence the German phrase "einem das Blut aussaugen," which translated means "to suck the goodness from the flour."

23. The exact method of peeling and sucking a fig, which Newton painfully detailed in his classic text, *Fig Cambridge*, has actually been recorded on film in Ken Russell's film adaptation of D.H. Lawrence's misogynistic novel, *Women in Love*. Alan Bates, in the role of Birkin, follows Newton's directions superbly, thereby establishing himself as the prototypical fig peeler. Clearly, Bates' classic peeling would have made Newton proud.

24. This approach to economics, thought to be considered "voo-doo" by most legitimate economists, was raised from the dead almost a century-and-a-half later by Ronald Reagan, who became President of the United States by advocating the same economic philosophy, thus confirming Graham's genius.

25. "Once upon a midnight dreary while I pondered weak and weary over many a quaint and curious volume of forgotten lore, while I nodded nearly napping suddenly there came a tapping, of someone gently rapping, rapping at my chamber door." The truth is, the tapping at the chamber door was not, in fact, a raven, but a delivery boy from a well-known Baltimore eatery called *Ameche's*, owned by one-time Colt running back Alan "The Horse" Ameche. Poe, like Proust, spent an inordinate amount of time indoors; unlike Proust, it was due in large measure to his wife's illness. Because of her inability to leave, Poe often ordered out for food. Journal entries indicate that the order for that day consisted of an Ameche Burger (with cheese), a cola, French fries, and, for dessert, Italian water ice, the eatery's specialty.

26. It is generally agreed upon that while living in Martinsville, Poe completed or started a number of works, not the least of which was his classic essay, "The Philosophy of Composition."

27. *The Collected Letters of Racine.* Paris: Jouir Press, 1996.

28. Actually, he said, "Elle est bien roulée," but it has somehow been altered in translation.

29. Krochleffel had made his fortune in the burger and pasta business and then began to diversify into real estate and film. His best-known film was the 1930 box-office hit *Caspar Milquetoast.*

30. *Hollywood*, Charles Bukowski. Original manuscript, p. 328.

31. Curiously, this particular attitude was revivified almost 60 years later in the 1994 California Gubernatorial Election as Proposition 187. A former California Governor, a long-time Céline aficionado and co-translator of *Bagatelles pour un massacre* (with noted Orange County xenophobe and jingoist Barbara Coe) privately coined the proposition, "the Céline Measure" as an homage to the ex-governor's hero. Unfortunately, the proposition passed, proving first that Ionesco's Rhinoceros was alive and well and running rampant in Southern California; second, the Newt Gingrich era of intolerance to the other was on the march; and third, much of Southern California and Italy had a number of things in common: fine wines, temperate climates, and a passing fancy for electing fascist legislators. Beranger could not be reached for comment. Word is he is now living in the Boundary Waters of Minnesota since Rhinos cannot endure the cold.

32. This name was, of course, an alias for Josef Mengele who assumed the identity of Koenigsburg thanks to the CIA who scuttled him out of Germany along with Albert Speer and Werner Von Braun in a VW minibus (later auctioned at Sotheby's and purchased by a representative of David Bowie) after the fall of Berlin. CIA memos on the subject indicate that Speer and Von Braun said they were going to the United States "to take their chances." Since Von Braun was a scientist, he felt he could have it "cushy just by creating designer bombs." Speer, on the other hand, thought he could use his architectural expertise to create what he called the "malling of America." Von Braun corrected Speer's English and suggested that what he meant to say was the "mauling of America." Speer replied, no, but, he added, they both amounted to the same thing. Mengele, on the other hand, said he "butchered and burned too many kike babies" to seek safe haven in the United States and opted instead for the Cono Sur. And though he eventually ended up in Bolivia, along with the remains of Butch Cassidy and the Sundance Kid, it wasn't before he had made a "killing" in the South American leather trade.

33. In a letter from Joyce to Dujardin, Joyce writes that without Dujardin's work, *Ulysses* would have been "a shipwrecked novel on the Iffey." Most Joycean scholars believe, and rightly, that Joyce was prompted by fellow Irishman Moore to write Dujardin and buoy his spirits since no one actually thought the novel was very innovative at any rate.

34. *Celebrity and the Press: From Kipling to Nixon.* Washington, D.C.: Neutered Books, 1985.

35. *Jungle Fever: The Roosevelt-Kipling Letters.* New York: Bully Books, 1952.

36. *Marie-Couche-Toi-Là: The Biography of Henri Menottes.* Paris: Coucherie Press, 1952.

37. Falla, "Notes sur Ravel," trans. Roland-Manuel, La Revue Musicale (March 1939), p. 83.

38. Ironically, these are the same boots Gable wore in the film, *Gone with the Wind*.

39. *Camille Claudel's Glass Menagerie.* Rainer Marie Rilke. Berlin: Weltschmerz Verlag, 1917.

40. *Tren Zich: Notes on Hitler and Mein Kampf.* Stockholm: Svenska Förlag, 1940.

41. It is a little known fact that when Andersen sold the rights to *The Little Mermaid* to the Disney Company™ he was told he could not write the script, but that the company would do everything in its power to remain "faithful to the integrity of the story." It was with Disney™ money that Andersen opened the famous Copenhagen café that bears his name and which was the site of so many heated arguments between Andersen and Kierkegaard, over whether or not he should have sold the rights.

42. *François Villon*. D.B. Wyndham Lewis. New York: Literary Guild of America, 1928.

43. By all accounts, Chermoye did not die of the stab wounds inflicted by Villon, but through lack of proper medical treatment. Apparently, Chermoye was directed to a local Paris HMO, which refused to stitch the priest since "he wasn't covered for thread and needle." Within the week he had died from a massive bacterial infection.

44. *C'est Une Autre Paire des Manches*. Michel Peteur. Paris: Gallimard et fils, 1867.

45. It was, of course, the Indianapolis Balzac's Balls franchise that sold the now defunct American Basketball Association on the idea of using tri-colored balls for the league; however, when the two leagues merged, the ball was dropped, so to speak, only to be picked up for use in the WNBA. Unfortunately for Balzac, there were no residuals.

46. The typewriter was purchased by William Frank Beckett, Beckett's grandfather, who, on a trip to Norwich, happened to visit the store and was impressed by the array of goods on sale.

47. Bustos Domecq was hired by Borges and Bioy-Casares, co-owner of the shop, as the cleaning person for the agency. After several years there, Domecq went on to have a rather distinguished writing career himself while continuing his janitorial duties.

48. As a matter of fact, the only recent translation of his play, *The Marvelous Pageant*, by Marcello Ejevarilla and Carmen Alicia del Campo, has also been rejected by over a dozen regional theatres throughout the United States and Canada. Given the relative indifference to his plays when he was alive, this news would not have greatly upset Cervantes.

49. The reason for the release of the long-sequestered notes is that Hemingway actually shared a semi-private room with one Doris Sokoloff, a married mother of two young sons, 14 and 9, who, though in the Mayo Clinic for the same reasons as Hemingway, was not treated with the same respect or dignity nor given the same medical attention as the *maestro*. Because of the scathing critical comments Hemingway wrote related to how she was mistreated (not to mention misdiagnosed) at the clinic, all of his notes were kept in a Rochester, Minnesota bank vault until recently, when Mayo attorneys, convinced there would be no malpractice litigation should the notes go public (the statute of limitations having since expired), released them for publication. The entire collection of Hemingway's notes will be published by Scribner's in a book titled *Hemingway's Mayo Papers,* set for a Spring, '05 release.

50. *The Séances of Victor Hugo.* Paris: Flammarion, 1985.

51. The company, of course, was originally called "The Willie Company" and went on to become the present day Disney™ Studios.

52. Little did either Eisner or Hugo know that because of financial and technical problems the film wouldn't appear for another 120 years.

53. This may have been the case as any casual scrutinizing of the video jacket of *The Little Mermaid* would attest. Andersen's outrage at the video jacket even caught the attention of his nemesis, Kierkegaard, who actually came to Andersen's defense in a monograph titled, *Dømmer Selv! Til Selvprøvelse Samtiden anbefalet* or *Judge For Yourselves! Recommended to the present time for Self-Examination.*

54. The codicil indicated that on any merchandising of *The Hunchback of Notre-Dame,* Hugo rightfully would be given top billing. The codicil was read and approved by Mr. Eisner.

55. It is common knowledge that this particular issue was not only the inspiration for McCarthy, but for the institution of the U.S. Patriot Act, an act of such monumental paranoia that it would have made Lawrence proud.

56. *Notes from a Disabled Dancer: Nijinsky's Memoes to Himself.* Ann Arbor, MI: Ardis Publishers, 1968.